AVENGING THE EARL'S LADY

SONS OF THE SPY LORD

ALINA K. FIELD

HAVENLOCK PRESS

Cover Design Dar Albert of Wicked Smart Designs

Image Credits: Period Images

For all Late Bloomers
Everywhere

FOREWORD

He's the most irritating, inscrutable, insufferable lord in the kingdom.
Also nosy, managing, and manipulative, and a man who's made an art of revenge.
She ought to know better than to encourage his attentions.
But…he's rich, and when an impossible debt from her past comes due, theft seems the only answer.

CHAPTER ONE

*S*he ought to know better than to encourage the attentions of the most meddlesome lord in the kingdom.

Lady Jane Montfort stretched on a sofa in the small library, trying vainly to snatch a few moments of much-needed sleep. Outside, the sea crashed and pounded, the din circling this snug Yorkshire cottage and slipping in through the half open window, as relentless as the rumbling male voices floating across the parlor from the council of spies in the dining room.

When another muffled drumming joined in, she rose and pushed the wood sash higher.

A sharp wind rushed her, far too chilling for the late July morning. No one was visible on the lane leading to Gorse Point Cottage, but there was no mistaking the hard-pounding hooves. A rider was coming.

She tiptoed through the parlor to the heavy wood entrance door and paused.

"I shall have to seduce information from her myself, then?"

The Spy Lord's deep baritone rolled out from the meeting room, the sound slithering up her spine, at once chilling and warming, sending her nerves tapping to match the other noises.

The Earl of Shaldon would casually try to seduce another woman for information, would he? Well, she supposed he'd been doing that all over Great Britain and the Continent since King Louis lost his head.

And if she had a drum—one of those small military ones would do—she'd crash it down upon Shaldon's firm-jawed, handsome head, ripping to shreds the taut leather or linen or bloody whatever else was stretched over the hoop.

The massive front door didn't so much as squeak when she stepped out. As she gulped in a great breath of the salty, moist air, the rider came into view, long-legged and plainly dressed. She couldn't discern if he was a mere messenger or one more of Shaldon's operatives galloping here at the Earl's behest.

Anger bubbled up in her. Except for Shaldon's daughter, Lady Perpetua, they were *all* here at the Earl's behest. But like Lady Perry, she herself was most certainly neither servant nor operative.

No, Shaldon was a handsome, enticing, and skilled manipulator, and so here she was, caught up in his schemes and blasted temptations while she had other matters, pressing matters, *personal* matters, to attend to.

She swallowed the moisture leaking down her throat. He'd *kissed* her mere hours ago. He'd *fondled* parts of her body that had been sleeping for more than two decades. Heavens, he'd all but seduced her in the stable yard, and she, an aging spinster, had been naught but a willing victim.

More fool her.

One of Shaldon's men came around from the back of the

house and took the reins while the rider dismounted and tossed his bag over his shoulder. Words were exchanged. The messenger shook his head and hurried to the front door.

He doffed his cap to reveal an abundance of glorious red hair. "My lady."

He knew her, but she didn't recognize him. He wasn't one of the Shaldon House servants. She knew all of them.

Behind her the air stirred. Warmth circled around her and pressed into her back, and she had to fight the urge to lean into it.

"Ah, Ewan, isn't it?" Shaldon said.

The Spy Lord himself had crept out of the door right behind her, and she hadn't even noticed.

Shaldon accepted a letter from the messenger, thankfully removing his hot hand from where it had trailed dangerously close to her backside, allowing her to breathe again.

"From my son, Gibson?" Shaldon asked.

The boy—for though he was tall, he was a lean, freckled thing—shook his head. "Mr. Gibson has loaned me to Lord Bakeley. He said to bring you this in all haste."

Jane's heart took another lurch. Shaldon's heir, Bakeley, and his wife, Lady Sirena, were expecting their first child. Only Shaldon's personal request that Jane travel to Yorkshire could have enticed her away from London and Lady Sirena.

And of course, there was the matter of Jane's dependency, living in Shaldon's elegant, well-appointed, well-staffed London residence. It was wise in those circumstances to go when one was sent.

"Is all well with them?" she asked.

The boy's wide-eyed look was enough of an answer to

that question. If Sirena was ill, Ewan didn't know of it. Except of course, being one of Shaldon's men, perhaps he wouldn't tell her anyway.

Ewan extended another letter. "My lady, I almost forgot. This one's for you."

The handwriting on the thick package was Sirena's. Dread knotted up in the pit of her stomach, flurries of worry making her hands tingle.

"Well, then." She nodded at both of them, dodging Shaldon's dark scrutiny. "I thank you for bringing it."

The letter bore Lady Sirena's handwriting, but the girl wouldn't send a missive this thick with news of the *ton* or the latest fashions. As Sirena would say, a fairy was whispering in Jane's ear, telling her that this letter was one more in a string of troubling messages.

It was appalling that one young man, so carefully brought up, so well provided for, could get himself into such a costly tangle, one that she'd been unraveling at no small expense.

She rushed in and took the stairs to the bedchamber she was sharing with Lady Perry.

A knock brought no answer, and so, she entered. The spring green counterpane was as smooth as it had been the morning before when she'd made up the bed. No one had slept there. Lady Perry had no doubt taken advantage of the previous night's chaos to visit the bed of her new fiancé, Fox.

She herself had spent the night in an armchair at Shaldon's bedside, taming her worries and her regrettable flutterings, and barely dozing between his bouts of nausea. By the time the dragoon captain's surgeon had come to examine him at daybreak, he'd recovered enough to call his council of old fools for a meeting.

His dosing of laudanum had worn off, and she'd escaped with not even a heated glance from his lordship.

She sighed and settled on the edge of the bed, studying the letter. Sirena's penmanship lacked elegance but it was clear and direct, like the girl herself.

The seal cracked neatly and she saw that the thick parchment surrounded another letter, its wax still in place. That letter's handwriting sent her nerves thrumming.

She took a deep breath, set the second letter aside, and unfolded Sirena's.

Dearest Jane,

I must dash this off quickly as Bakeley is at my elbow demanding all haste. Be assured that all is well with the babe and I am even deigning to take some of your advice. I've shortened my time in the saddle and I limit myself to a boring walk—no trotting or galloping! Bakeley accompanies me on every ride to ensure the safety of his heir.

You've likely heard the good news that Captain Kingsley is found and is on his way to England.

That was indeed wonderful news. Shaldon's other new daughter-in-law, Graciela, would be happy that her missing father had been found.

Though perhaps, Lord Shaldon being Lord Shaldon, he hasn't shared the news from the letter Bakeley sent him by the same courier. (And Dear Jane, must you keep running off with my father-in-law? First Bath, now Yorkshire; tongues will be wagging, though not mine, I assure you.) And, by the by, Mr. Oliver Morton drew me aside at last night's ball to inquire about your absence...

Her hand fisted around the paper. Sirena knew Jane had been called to Bath by her cousin and his ailing wife, playing the poor relation at yet another noble establishment. Shaldon might have *said* he was in Bath, but if he was, he hadn't been there to take the waters or mingle with polite society. He hadn't been there to make *her* heart flutter—perhaps he had a ladybird tucked away there, a spy or a French emigre from his past.

And Mr. Morton? Sirena's fey senses had picked up the man's interest, but she couldn't know the old goat had made Jane a grabby proposal of marriage. One she'd refused.

She smoothed the paper and read on.

I've enclosed a letter just delivered by messenger, unopened, though I confess, I was sorely tempted. The messenger asked that it be forwarded to you in all haste. I do hope all is well, and if it is not, you must apply to me for assistance, as I am now wife to a wealthy viscount and forever in your debt, dear friend. Never fear, I have ways of convincing Bakeley to part with his money.

Jane rubbed at the ache in her temple, stuck a loose lock of hair behind her ear, and read on.

Barton and Madame send their love. They are drowning in orders, poor dears, working from dawn until midnight, and Bakeley is quite smug about the success of his investment in their enterprise.

Do take care and come home soon. Without you and Perry, I am hopelessly lost running Shaldon House.

With love,

S

Dear Sirena, always so perceptive and so kind.

Asking her for help was a solution, one that was totally unacceptable. Her husband, Bakeley—Shaldon's heir—had generously invested in the partnership of Jane's former lady's maid and a French modiste, and with the new King's coronation festivities in full swing, he was seeing a good return.

There would be no return on any money given to her.

She would simply be sinking to the utter, humiliating charity she had managed to avoid her entire life.

Besides, Bakeley would want to know why she needed it.

She weighed the sealed letter in her hand, the *tap-tap-tap* on her nerves growing more insistent. With her even-tempered and orderly man of business, *all haste* was a rarity. All haste was grounds for a whole host of fairies to plague her.

The shakiness of the script reminded her that she should be thinking about a successor to Mr. Phillips, who worked with only a clerk as elderly as himself.

She cracked the wax wafer and scanned the lines, her heart sinking.

CHAPTER TWO

*M*oney was needed, a great deal more than previously thought, and a great deal more than she possessed.

My Dear Lady Jane,

I beg your forgiveness for disturbing you yet again during this busy time, but an urgent message arrived today from Mr. Walker that I must share with you. He has no wish to importune your noble personage, but the expectations of his ward exceed what the young man's income, and Mr. Walker's, will allow. The young man has confessed to Mr. Walker that his debts were substantially more than previously thought, so much so that he availed himself of professional money lenders. The additional sum, beyond what you have already provided from drawing on the principle of your aunt's bequest, has consequently grown with interest to almost one thousand pounds. To make matters worse, the debts have been sold to a certain individual who is demanding either repayment, or satisfaction.

Her heart pounded so loudly, she pressed the letter to her breast to settle it.

She'd known there was more debt, but not *this* much. She'd pondered a resolution: employment for him, an income that would cover quarterly payments to creditors. She'd even considered marriage—not for *him*, of course. No heiress would engage to marry a clergyman's ward of questionable birth.

Oliver Morton had offered for *her*, but he was unlikely to settle money on a new wife to pay off another man's debts.

She must find another way. She took a deep breath and read on.

Mr. Walker expressed that he believes a mere deposit of funds, if they can be found, will not be enough to ensure the young man understands the gravity of the course he is on. Mr. Walker himself is not well enough to come up to town and pay a personal visit to counsel him on his latest extravagances. He believes it is time for the young man to meet his noble benefactor in person.

My lady, I have kept your cousin, Lord Cheswick's, identity secret all of these years, as well as yours, and I am at a loss as to how to respond to Mr. Walker or how to advise managing this debt. We have drawn down almost to nil the funds left you by Lady Mildred. For the rest, your cousin would never allow touching the principle. Might you apply to him for a solution? I fear I must tell you that payment is expected a fortnight from yesterday.

I shall await your further instructions.

One thousand pounds? How was such an amount of money to be found?

But it must be found. If not, he would have to discard all honor and flee England, or fight a duel. Either choice was unthinkable.

"Ah, Jane, there you are." Lady Perry slipped into the

room, disheveled, but with a smile that spread from ear to ear above the ugly bruise that colored her neck, courtesy of the local baronet, Sir Richard Fenwick. Lady Perry had escaped from the man a few nights before, and he was now under guard in the Gorse Point Cottage stable.

She beat down her racing heart and folded away the solicitor's letter and its secrets. Shaldon had requested her presence in Yorkshire for the sole purpose of safeguarding Perry's reputation, and what a joke that was.

Still, mere whispers of scandal could ruin a lady's place in society, and for Perry's sake, she would persevere in her role as chaperone.

"Shall I ask where you slept last night, Lady Perry? No, perhaps I'd better not, inasmuch as your father hasn't raised a fuss."

Perry hurried over and hugged her. "Fox said Father will speak to him later today."

"Good. The sooner we get settlements arranged and the two of you married, the better."

The younger lady plopped down next to her, making the bed ropes creak. "Don't worry. Fox won't desert me."

"I wasn't thinking of desertion. This business he's involved in is dangerous." Given the risks inherent in Shaldon's activities, it was *death* she was thinking of, but she couldn't bring herself to shatter the girl's glow with that word. A lady must hang on to moments of happiness.

"Painting pictures?" Perry scoffed. "I suppose he might catch the oils on fire if he works late at night with a candle close by."

She gritted her teeth. "It's the business he conducts for your father that concerns me."

"I know." Perry patted her hand. "I knew what you meant. I oughtn't tease after all that has happened the last few days. But surely, with Sir Richard captured, this assignment, or whatever it is, is over, and Fox may get on with becoming the most famous artist in all of England, married to the outrageously wealthy daughter of an earl."

Jane studied her. Laughter sparkled in Perry's eyes, and she glowed with the happiness of mutual love. She'd most certainly spent the night with Fox.

Perry was wealthy, or would be, when she married. She might convince her new husband, who was not so nosy and high in the instep as Bakeley, to let her help Jane, but even if they married by Special License, she might not get access to funds soon enough.

And Jane couldn't importune the girl, not after everything she'd gone through the last few days.

There was little more she could do for Perry. She should make her way back to London and the problems awaiting her there.

"Your father will surely keep Fox out of harm's way until after the nuptials. And in any case, no matter what might happen, your brothers will always help you. Though you did run away from one of them."

"I wanted to see this house that will be mine someday. And I truly did not know Fox was here. And, I don't believe Father plans to talk to him about settlements. I think it's about the painting."

"The painting?"

"Yes. The one we carried back last night from Sir Richard's. Did you look at it?"

A glimpse of it had left an impression of a dark, dismal, rather ugly work.

"Oh, it's dreadfully distressed, but it's supposedly a masterpiece by a Spanish artist who worked in the new world." Perry flung out a hand. "You don't know the story, of course you wouldn't. Father got hold of it who-knows-how many years ago and gave it to my mother. The Martyrdom of Saints Perpetua and Felicity. Mother loved it, it being *a-thing-of-value*, and her being a *Felicity*. Thus, she settled me with my ridiculous name...but, however Father obtained it, someone else coveted it. When Father was captured in Spain, Mother sent the painting as part of the ransom demand."

The hair on Jane's neck quivered. *Shaldon had been captured in Spain? The painting had been sent as a ransom to someone who coveted it?*

A fog lifted. Of course. Shaldon had spent the years since the end of the war on a quest for revenge against one old enemy or another. He must be tracking down his captors.

"Who held your father, Perry?"

"The Duque de San Sebastian."

The Duque de San Sebastian? Weeks earlier at a diplomatic ball, an unpleasant scene had played out between the Duque and Shaldon.

Perry stood and began to pace. "Yes. And with the Duque in London, it's a wonder Father doesn't kill him outright. In any case, before my mother sent the painting, she had Fox copy it. And then, at the last minute, she decided to send the copy and keep the original."

Jane's breath caught. Perry's mother had died years ago, and she hadn't known her well. The few times they'd met, the lady had been kind enough to her, a much younger girl.

But gambling her husband's life for a painting?

"Does your father know?"

"Yes, or, at least I think so. Fox had a few moments alone with him last night when you went for fresh linens."

She crumpled the letters, images from the night before whirling—Shaldon bloodied and beaten, but not broken, never that. Last night, before they'd left Sir Richard's, Shaldon had backed her alone into a corner. He'd unleashed more marvelous passion than she'd felt in years.

Why had his wife risked losing him?

She shook off a spark of anger. "And it fell into Sir Richard's hands."

"Yes, after he killed Mother, he took it."

Perry's matter-of-factness sent a shiver through her.

"It's shocking, I know," Perry said, plopping down again. "I'm relieved to know the truth of what happened. No one would tell me anything, other than that she died in a terrible carriage accident."

Jane's nerves clacked again, a great yawning hole in her heart opening. She also had once been spared the full details of a family tragedy. It had not been a kindness.

She eased in a breath. "Did the copy pass for the original? Your father was released, was he not?"

"No. The Duque had never planned to free him. When Fox delivered the painting—"

"*Fox?*"

"Yes. Fox was the courier, and *he* was imprisoned as well, and then the Duque turned them both over to the French. Father escaped and went back to rescue Fox."

No wonder Shaldon was letting the American artist marry his only daughter.

"For years, I wondered if Fox was a thief. He left Cransdall a few days before my mother and the painting vanished. And then she left and never came home." Perry took a deep breath. "Mother always told me she meant me to inherit the painting, but Father hasn't mentioned that, and I don't care a bit about it, even if it *is* priceless, as Fox says. I don't wish for the Duque to have it, though."

She squeezed Perry's hand.

"Fox told me the Duque treated Father quite badly. Father is after revenge."

Jane sighed. "Of course he is." For Shaldon, the fighting had never ended. He'd continued on, he and his man, Kincaid, chasing after old enemies and pulling his children into the troubles. Behind that handsome facade, he was all twisted up in his need to settle old scores. And what an utter waste of time it was.

A scratching at the door brought the maid, Jenny.

"I'm to help you start packing, Lady Perry," she said.

"Packing?" Perry said.

The girl nodded. "His lordship says you're to leave tomorrow for London."

Perry shot to her feet. "Tomorrow?" She plopped her hands on her hips.

Once they returned to Shaldon House and the watchful eyes of the staff, Perry might not have the freedom to sneak into Fox's bed.

"I for one, will be glad to get back," Jane said. "And I suppose, Fox will visit Doctor's Commons so you can marry with a Special License."

Perry chewed on her lip, nodding.

Jenny coughed. "Mr. Fox was to stay here, I heard his lordship say. Him and Mr. Kincaid, and you, Lady Jane, to look after Mr. Kincaid until he heals enough to travel."

Her face grew warm, her fingers again curled around the letters.

Would he try to break up the engagement he'd just approved? Perry might even now be with child—one night of passion was enough for *that*. As for herself...the letters in her hand reminded her she needed to return to London immediately.

And somehow, secure a thousand pounds.

She smoothed out the paper and took in a breath. She had no one she could turn to for the funds. Her cousin Cheswick had stood by her in her very worst years, agreeing to her plans and supplementing her inheritance, allowing her the life she'd pleaded for. With estates and tenants, and his own children to raise, he was too cash-strapped to offer much more than hospitality, even if she dared to ask it, and as her solicitor had said, he'd never allow her to touch the principle of her accounts that were under his control. If he knew she'd withdrawn from Great Aunt Mildred's bequest, he would think she'd been reckless.

There was Sirena, like herself, the daughter and cousin of an earl. Sirena had served as Jane's companion in the humble rooms they'd taken upon their arrival in London last year, before they'd both moved into the large Shaldon townhouse in Mayfair.

But if Sirena learned her secret, Bakeley would also, and surely then Shaldon would find out.

Shaldon, the man who'd taken her into his home, the man who'd kissed her yesterday, expected her to stay here and nurse the blasted man she'd stitched up twice because the fool would not stay put. She couldn't bear to have Shaldon discover this piece of her past. There was no telling how he'd use it against her.

She wouldn't seek charity that would destroy friendships, nor would she sell herself into a loathsome marriage.

Enough dithering—she'd sell what she had of value, and for the rest, she'd do what she must.

"No," Perry said, pulling her out of her thoughts. "That won't do. The coronation is in days and Jane wants to attend the parties. I don't give two shakes about them."

God's truth, the joy had gone out of the coronation

celebration. The money she'd eked out for gowns would go to a different use now, and she'd have to find a great deal more, and soon, by whatever means necessary.

She'd seen a Limoges vase in this parlor and some quality books in the small library. All of this would be Lady Perry's upon her marriage and perhaps she'd understand.

Jane would take them to London and seek Barton's and Madame's help selling them.

But...the items would be the devil to carry, and she would not like to travel alone.

"And what of you, Jenny? Are you to accompany Lady Perry?" The sensible little maid had been Perry's companion in her flight to freedom.

The girl blinked. "His lordship didn't say."

Perry's gaze met Jenny's. "Lady Jane will need you more."

"I would like that," Jane said.

Jenny could stay here with her, and then what? She couldn't involve the girl in her plotting...in her theft. If caught and prosecuted, she might get transportation at the worst, but Jenny would hang.

She stood and began to pace. She must think this through. She needed money, and she needed to make haste to London and...

The painting. It was a Spanish masterpiece. A thing of value, Perry had said, a painting that was to have been hers, and one she didn't care about. Not hard to carry if one rolled it up. And if one rich man wanted it badly, others would also. Jane had heard whispers that Madame's cousin dealt in such matters.

Dear God. Shaldon had not given the painting to his daughter yet. Steal it from Shaldon, not Perry? Perhaps he wouldn't prosecute, but he'd chase her to the farthest corners of the world to get back what was his.

But if Lady Shaldon wanted her daughter to have it, then technically she'd be stealing from Perry, who didn't want the painting and would surely understand, as long as Jane didn't sell it to the Duque.

She shoved the letters into her pocket, found her Kashmiri shawl, and pulled it around her. It had been her brother's last gift and wrapping herself in the vibrant reds and oranges of the rich print always brought him closer.

She'd considered selling the shawl if she must. But the painting was so much more valuable.

Would Shaldon leave it here at Gorse Point Cottage?

"What of the painting, Jenny?" she asked. "Did his lordship say whether he is taking it?"

"No, milady."

Perry's gaze narrowed. "Why?"

Her chest squeezed and she gulped for air. "I wondered. You said it was quite valuable."

Perry shook her head. "Quite valuable to the right buyer. You must tell me what you're thinking."

What she was thinking?

She waved a hand. "Mere nonsense. I was...thinking about Sirena. About what she would say. She'd say the painting was cursed. She'd say whoever transported it might...might bring bad luck with them."

That nonsense tale was good enough to make Perry laugh.

And when had Lady Jane Montfort ever been so quick with a lie? She'd always been far more ponderous in her plotting.

"If you're worried about Father's safety traveling with it, you mustn't be. But I'll find out his plans for it. Fox will tell me. Where are you going?"

"I need some fresh air. I'm going for a walk. Alone."

. . .

A FEW MINUTES EARLIER

In the dining room, Edward Everly, Earl of Shaldon, poured another cup of coffee and studied the letter spread before him.

"Is Kingsley well?" Kincaid asked.

He smoothed the paper. "Bakeley doesn't say. He's aboard a British naval vessel and will be arriving in Portsmouth within the month."

"Good that he's returning," Kincaid said. "What has the able privateer found, I wonder?"

"Nothing he would entrust to a letter."

"We'd best set a stout guard when we take the painting down to London."

"The best place for it is Cransdall." His country estate was well protected, and the painting had hung on the wall of his wife's bedchamber there for many years.

He glanced at the sideboard. Since its removal decades ago from New Spain, it hadn't fared well. His late wife, Felicity, had held off restoring it, fearing it would lose value. Always one to consider the price of things, was Felicity.

It had arrived in England rolled up on a privateer's ship, and ten years ago, Fox had rolled it again for transporting. The paint had cracked in places, and Fenwick's care had not involved any more than reframing.

And the fool hadn't known what he'd had in that frame.

"Did Felicity know the true value?" Kincaid asked.

He shook his head. He'd not known the painting's secrets himself when he'd presented it to her as a gift early in their marriage. As he'd suspected, she was delighted with the subject matter of the painting—and its intrinsic value as a masterpiece. Had she known more she would have funded her own explorations. "No. Among us, only the two of us, Farnsworth, and Kingsley. And San Sebastian, of course."

"And whoever wrote down the coordinates," Kincaid said. "I wonder if Fox copied the markings accurately?" Kincaid rubbed at his bandaged chest. "Probably not, else San Sebastian would not still be looking for missing treasure. Is there aught else of import in Bakeley's letter?"

"Plans for the coronation are proceeding accordingly." And the King was demanding his return to London, in all haste, for the honor of scraping and bowing with his fellow peers who were escorting the latest George to his throne.

The maid peeked in and he waved her over. "I must hasten back to London, Kincaid. King's orders. You'll stay here. Ewen and Lady Jane can stay as well and see to you, and Fox can provide an extra hand should there be trouble from the squire's smuggling associates. Girl, go and pack Lady Perpetua's things and inform her that we'll leave at first light tomorrow. And have someone look for Fox."

The girl curtsied and left.

"Neither lady will like this," Kincaid said.

He eyed his old friend. They'd both been through hell the previous two days, but Kincaid was the worse for wear.

"Get yourself back to bed, Kincaid, and heal up. I'll need you when we move against San Sebastian."

Kincaid got to his feet grunting. "Your lady took too much pleasure in poking me with a needle. I've a feeling she might bolt."

His lady? Pleasure stirred fiercely in him and he eased in a breath, fighting for composure. The blasted laudanum was still in his system. "Placid, staid, dependable Jane?" She'd shown great courage the previous night and more than a little answering passion.

Kincaid smirked, shook his head, and left.

Shaldon let out a breath. The laudanum administered by Sir Richard to keep him under control in his captivity had never had the effect of making him a randy fool before, though perhaps he hadn't had the right lady as inspiration.

He glanced at the letter again. The one Jane received had been much thicker. He'd recognized his daughter-in-law's handwriting, and Bakeley had mentioned he was forwarding a letter from her solicitor, though not the details of its contents.

But the letter had alarmed Jane. He'd seen the sharp intake of breath that'd sent her breasts higher.

They were fine breasts, too, not weighed down by years of childbearing. She'd kept her youth and her figure, but the price had been living meekly, hand to mouth, and on the charity of others.

She was the daughter of an earl—why the devil had her cousin never found her a husband? A marriage of convenience was the usual refuge for an earl's daughter, and most couples found a way to muddle through the match-up.

His stomach churned and his gaze went again to the rectangle of painted canvas that had been unmounted to check for the markings. It would be the devil to stretch and put back together.

He would leave that task to Fox while he himself answered the King's summons.

In any case, London was where his last prey was: the Duque de San Sebastian. The Duque, who thought he'd received *this* painting. But all the while, it had been hanging in Sir Richard Fenwick's bedchamber.

Because Shaldon's late wife, Felicity, had betrayed him.

The ache in his shoulder from the previous day's injuries spread to the back of his neck.

A flash of red and gold in the window caught his eye. He

shoved out of his chair and moved to the curtain. Jane was swathed in the exotic shawl she often wore and heading down the path that snaked around to the back of the cottage. That way led to the cliff road.

She'd been up all night...even for someone well-rested and steady, the cliff road could be dangerous.

CHAPTER THREE

*T*he rocks crunched under her boots and the damp breeze crept under her wrap as she hurried down the stone stairs at the side of the house.

Gorse Point Cottage perched on the cliff, four levels stacked up the hillside, with the ground floor kitchen opening into a stable yard that stretched on a small, flat plateau before the hill broke off again into boulders.

A soldier stood a weary duty in front of the stables, and one of Shaldon's men circled the rock-bound yard, keeping an eye out for trouble.

They didn't so much as acknowledge her. Each year she'd become less and less visible. She'd soon be able to walk through the world of men completely unseen.

No wonder she'd almost succumbed to the Earl's attempt on her dubious virtue.

The road curved around boulders and gorse-thickened outcrops. Lady Perry had explained the layout and roads two nights ago. This lane would lead on until it reached a highway that led west to the Earl of Shaldon's home at Cransdall, the grand country estate that she'd never visited.

Her own route up from London had skirted north past Scarborough on a different road. She'd traveled at all speed in Shaldon's sleek chaise, days and nights of poor or no sleep and no thoughts but the need to preserve Lady Perry's reputation, and then, when she'd arrived, no thought but to save Shaldon's life.

And now, she had no thought but to steal from the man.

Rounding a bend, she reached a straight stretch, and the sight of it sent her heart pounding. The edge of the road sheered off from a path so narrow, if a wagon approached it might not be able to squeak by her.

Leagues below her, the wild North Sea waters crashed against jagged rocks, beating, withdrawing, regrouping, and coming back for more. Patient and persistent, for eons, the sea had chipped away at this coast.

It was much like the coastline near her father's estate in Kent. The rocks poking up from below sent her head spinning, pushing the air from her lungs.

"Careful."

She jumped, and a hand gripped her arm, steadying her. Shaldon's dark gaze pierced her, sending heat sparking in waves. In spite of his age, in spite of the trials of the past two days, he was still virile, still vital.

What did he want with a middle-aged spinster like herself? He could go back to the marriage mart, catch a young girl's eye, and start on another crop of handsome boys.

Hadn't he once caught her own eye when she was a young girl in Kent?

How old would he be? He'd fathered his first child, an illegitimate son, in Ireland before reaching the age of twenty. Past fifty then, and yet only a bit of gray streaked over his ears. And he was still stealthy as a cat when he wanted to be. Not so much as a pebble had shifted under his boots when he'd crept up behind her.

She tucked the shawl tighter around her, shaking off his hand in the process. "It's a grand view, isn't it?"

"It's perilous," he said. "You shouldn't be here."

"You are right, of course," she said. "Yet you did ask me to come."

He sighed. "I meant, you shouldn't be on this road."

Her face heated. If she must hie off to Yorkshire at a moment's notice, if she must stay and nurse his henchman, she'd walk where she wanted.

She strolled on, and he came up beside her.

"This is where my lady wife died."

Pulse pounding, she stopped. It was naught but stone wall on one side and a rock ledge, and sheer cliff on the other.

"This very spot?"

"So I was told."

"H-how? Did not Sir Richard murder her?"

"Yes."

She let out a sharp breath. "She went over?"

"He picked her up and threw her over."

He'd punched every word from a well of anger, though his face remained eerily calm. Frightening, this man could be, and indomitable. She could see why his children resisted him…and how he still steered them around to his way. And how he managed other members of his household, like herself.

He was like the waves below. He would crash and withdraw, and rise up to crash again. He would never stop.

If she stole from him, she'd pay a price.

"I'm sorry." She mumbled the words by rote, unable to unscramble her emotions.

Pain stabbed her chest and sent moisture to her eyes, and she took a step back into the stone wall. Her brother had died on a beach below rocks like this, and her brother's friend, Reginald, also. Shaldon had been there that night, a part of the unsolved riddle of what happened to the two younger men. Shaldon had been there, and somehow, he and his indomitable will had been involved, though Father would never explain how.

She sucked in a breath. The time for mourning had long passed. She must live in the present, and to hell with the old pains that from time to time flared.

And to hell with worries about the future. She'd do what she must to fulfill her most sacred commitment.

"I'm sorry, "she repeated. "Such a trite phrase, but there it is." Best to push him off his guard. "And the painting? Sir Richard had the real one, not the copy?"

He raised an eyebrow.

"Perry told me the story."

"She should not have."

She shrugged and stepped out again. "If you want to lure the Duque de San Sebastian, you have the perfect instrument." She held her breath and waited for a cutting reply, but he only grunted, keeping pace with her.

"Bakeley wrote to me that Lady Sirena was forwarding an urgent letter from your solicitor."

Oh, that was so much worse than a cutting remark—he was turning the conversation back upon her and prying.

But she was not one of his children to be ruled and manipulated. "Yes, I have it," she said.

"I hope all is well."

"Hmm." He could hope until the sea rose up and washed away this road but she wouldn't discuss the matter with him. She'd kept her secrets for decades, as he had kept his.

"If you will stay and help Kincaid for a few days, I would greatly appreciate it. When Kincaid is able to travel, Bakeley will send someone to bring you to Shaldon House, if not in time for the coronation, then at least in good time for the festivities after."

He'd not bother himself with the task of organizing her return, he'd have his son Bakeley do it.

The heat rising in her now was not shock or embarrassment or grief.

She caught her breath again. Why should it matter to her who he sent?

She quickened her pace, and almost tripped on a jutting rock.

"Careful." He had her by the arm again.

"This road needs maintaining," she said.

"It is seldom used."

"Perhaps now, with Lady Perry marrying, she and Fox will see to it."

He tucked her hand over his arm, drawing her closer. "Perhaps it's time you see to your future, Jane."

Excitement pulsed through her as she remembered the feel of his lips on hers the night before, his hand caressing her. What if...Her throat went dry.

"Mr. Morton has made a good offer," he said.

Breath *whooshed* from her. She was a fool. And how could Shaldon possibly know about Oliver Morton's offer of marriage?

A large series of waves thundered below them while she fought for her breath, fought for enough saliva to make her tongue work, finally lifting her gaze to his. "Was that offer your idea then, Lord Shaldon?"

Is it more of your matchmaking? Does Morton have a spy in his wardrobe who you're after?

She held his gaze, watching him. Oh, he was good. Perfectly impassive.

"He spoke to me," he said, finally.

"Which doesn't answer the question posed."

A long implacable silence followed. She waited him out again.

"What you must think of me, Jane." He swiped a hand through his hair. "No. He merely asked my thoughts on the match."

"I see."

She did. She was living in Shaldon's household. She had become one of his retainers. One of his responsibilities. One of his many properties.

She would not return to Shaldon House. It was just as well. Once she'd stolen the painting, she'd have the devil of a time concealing her theft if she was right under the man's nose.

She pulled her arm free yet again. "I shall consider your advice, my lord. Good day."

He would leave tomorrow morning, and she would ponder the best time for her own departure, how she would go about committing her crime, and who she might get to take her in after all of her quarterly funds were spent.

She headed back to the cottage, setting a fast pace, his steps no longer quiet but echoing hers the entire way.

SHALDON WATCHED HER TENSE BACK AND HER TAUT STEP AND caught up with her in the stable yard, escorting her to the kitchen door. She wished him another good day before crossing the threshold, ever so calm, ever so polite.

And inside, seething, and wishing him to the devil. Lady Jane Montfort was the quintessential genteel lady. One with money problems, else why would the solicitor be writing in urgency? And for God's sake, over what? She didn't gamble. She didn't run up her bills at the shops.

He oughtn't to have mentioned Morton, but he couldn't help wanting to see her reaction. The man had sought him out, speculating that Shaldon had an interest in Jane, making sure his proposal would offer no offense to an earl.

The implication, of course, was that he was keeping Jane in his home as his mistress. He ought to have tossed the man out on his ear for the insult to her. Besides which, Morton was seventy if he was a day, the toothless old bugger. He'd try to hold Jane on a short lease, and he'd undoubtedly scrimp on her pin money.

The match was distasteful. Jane would be shortchanged, no matter how Morton bragged about his member still working.

He shook off that thought and spotted the dragoon captain heading for the stables.

"How is our prisoner?" he asked.

"He'll have a few days in him before the festering bullet takes him. Possibly longer."

"Has he talked?"

"No, but the others have. That devil we transported last year wasn't your smuggling king, John Black. The real John Black is lying up inside here. This will gut the free traders around here for a while."

"A short while. Others will rise up."

"Aye, as long as there's taxes, there's smuggling. There's the pity, but it means my men and I will have work."

The captain was a sanguine, intelligent fellow. He gave a sharp salute and left to check on his prisoner.

When the stable door opened, another one of his stalwart old comrades, Lord Farnsworth, slipped out and joined him. The kitchen door swung quietly as they entered, but the sharp little maid looked up from the pot she was stirring.

"Is your kettle hot?" Shaldon asked.

She scuttled around scooping tea while he and Farnsworth took seats at the scarred table.

"Are we settled then on the plan?" he asked Farnsworth.

The girl's hand shook hefting the heavy pot. She wasn't a kitchen drudge—the chit had risen in the servant ranks to serve each of his sons' wives and then Lady Perpetua, and she was a loyal thing. Every word they spoke here would be reported back to his stubborn daughter and Jane. Jenny, this sly little one from the Seven Dials, had proved a formidable ally for the women.

"Yes," Farnsworth said, "the plan is well in place." He glanced at the girl as she set out the cups. "I see all the rolling pins are still festooning the kitchen. Have you had occasion to use them, girl?"

An entire wall was hung with glass cylinders of every tint, painted with every scene imaginable—florals and oriental themes, stripes and solids, messages of love. Purely decorative now.

A memory flooded him, of a week he'd spent here with Felicity, just the two of them, huddled in this kitchen, living on buttered bread and cold meats. He'd sneaked back to England to recuperate from some wound or other and meet with his government contact, and Felicity had shared the story of these ornaments.

"No, sir." the girl said. "They're too pretty to use. Lady Jane thought so too."

"They belonged to my late wife's grandmother," he said. "Those rolling pins came to England filled with salt."

Farnsworth smiled. "Duty free."

His wife's wealth had come from banking, but the bank had been staked with the profits from smuggling.

They weren't filled with salt now, but perhaps they would still have some value.

He turned to the maid. "Tell Lady Jane she may take whichever ones she wishes with her when she leaves, with my blessing."

"Yes, milord."

"And did I not tell you to start packing my daughter's things for tomorrow?"

"It won't take but a moment to pack for us, milord."

"You'll stay here. Lady Jane and Fox will need you to prepare meals."

The girl colored. "To be honest, milord, Mr. Fox has done most of the cooking. I don't know much more than boiling water for tea."

Farnsworth took a sip. "But it's a fine job you've done with it. We'll get in some bread and things from the village so old Kincaid doesn't starve. Do you suppose Lady Jane knows her way a bit around the kitchen?"

"She might," Shaldon said. "And if she's hungry enough, she'll learn along with you, girl."

He downed his cup and handed it to the maid. "Farnsworth, let's go up and have a look at the statement from Fenwick."

* * *

WHEN THE INNER DOOR THAT LED TO THE STAIRS CLOSED, Jane slipped out of the storeroom with the wheel of cheese she'd gone to collect.

"Oh, my lady," Jenny whispered.

The girl's pity made Jane's eyes moisten.

Blinking hard, she plopped the cheese down on the board. "So, it's to be you and me, Jenny, hungry enough to find our way around the kitchen." She grabbed a great carving knife and slammed it into the wedge.

The blade stuck there like King Arthur's sword. She had been hungry moments before. Now...

She blinked some more and eased in a breath. Patience. Shaldon was right, wasn't he? A hungry woman would find her way in the kitchen, even if she was an earl's daughter. She didn't want to be one of Shaldon's retainers. She didn't want to be in his care and keeping.

"I don't believe I've broken my fast this morning, Jenny. I'm glad we had this cheese put aside."

A chunk of this cheese would go with her when she left. She had some money for the journey—she always made certain of that. And she could ask Perry to loan her more. Or perhaps Shaldon's credit would carry her through the nearest villages. Or she could insist he leave extra money on the pretense of purchasing more food.

Jenny slid a steaming cup to her.

She forced a smile. "I'm glad for your company here, Jenny." Her gaze caught the wall of painted glass cylinders. "I can take whichever of these I want, he said."

"They're pretty," Jenny said. "How ever will you carry them without them breaking?"

Her breath calmed more, glad for the reminder to be practical. Perhaps the girl might be willing to run away with her.

"I'll cushion them with garments. They are lovely. I feel an urge to be selfish and take more than one."

"Would they fetch a good price, do you think? Not as I would ever think of taking them, milady. I'm not a thief."

She glanced at the girl. There'd been no irony in her

voice. Being accused of theft must be a real concern for a servant girl with her background. "No, of course not, Jenny."

She studied the cylinders and took one off the wall. Gold paint snaked all around in an intricate pattern of leaves and vines. It was one of many, stuck away here in this remote Yorkshire cottage gathering dust. The lady who'd loved and valued them was long dead.

"His Lordship said I might take what I want, but he didn't say I have to keep them. With the right buyer, this one, for example, might fetch enough money to carry me, or perhaps both of us, all the way back to London."

They wouldn't fetch as much as she ultimately needed, but she would keep them in mind if she couldn't get her hands on something that would.

"I'm to stay, his lordship said."

The girl was beholden to Lord Shaldon, far more than Jane was. She wouldn't risk disobeying.

"But we might need to go into town ourselves for the foodstuffs." Jenny said. "A man might not know to check over the bread and make sure it's fresh. We've the cart Lady Perpetua and I arrived on, if you can drive it." She paused and pressed her lips together. "But, the cliff road, milady; even Lady Perpetua got off and led the horse on that road."

Jane yanked the blade out and sawed off a piece of cheese, her hopes rising. Jenny must know the cliff road didn't lead to the village. "I used to handle a gig when I was a girl. It has been some time since but I'm sure it will come back to me." She smiled and leaned in. "And we won't take that cliff road when we leave."

CHAPTER FOUR

*W*hen she carried a tray up that night for Kincaid, Shaldon was there at the bedside.

"If Kingsley has found that code's hidden treasure, he's kept mum," Shaldon said.

"On the other hand," Kincaid said, "his daughter's great dowry had to have come from—"

Kincaid spotted her in the doorway and hastily closed his mouth and pulled the sheet over his bandaged chest.

"Good evening, gentlemen." She set the tray on the small bedside table and bent over him before he could push himself up and reopen his wound.

"Just leave that dish and I'll get out of this bed—"

"Stop squirming, Mr. Kincaid. We'll raise you up. Lord Shaldon, go around to the other side and help me please."

"I'll not—"

"If I'm to be your nurse for the next several days, you'll do as I say. And you, my lord, your strong arm is needed."

"One of the boys—"

"Can help with your privy needs, but I'm to be feeding you and checking your bandage."

Shaldon, miraculously, had heeded her instructions and was slipping an arm under Kincaid's broad back. She propped Kincaid's other shoulder, making sure to keep her hand out of Shaldon's reach.

Kincaid grimaced as she plumped his pillows.

"The stitches are pulling, are they?" she asked. "I see a spot of blood or two. Your bandage will need changing."

"The surgeon can do it," Kincaid said.

"The surgeon has gone along the coast. He won't be back until tomorrow or after. But very well. We'll have Ewan see to the bandage as well." She settled the tray over his lap and lifted a cover. "Stew."

"More like a plain beef tea."

"Which, considering how much you bled, would be good for you. But we've added some turnips and beef."

Shaldon had backed away from the bed and propped himself against the wall, his arms crossed in front of him.

Kincaid grumbled and picked up his spoon. Gray hair and freckles sprinkled his chest. It was the first male chest she'd seen in twenty years, and a fine muscular one it was. Seeing to Kincaid's wounds had reminded her even more of what she'd missed in her long years of spinsterhood.

But the sight of his chest completely failed to stir her.

"The maid could have brought up the dinner," Shaldon said.

His bored drawl rubbed on her patience. "You did ask her to see to packing Lady Perry's things."

He didn't need to know that the girl wasn't doing that. Perry had no intention to go on the morrow, not if she must leave without Fox.

Fox, for his part, was reluctant to anger his future father-in-law. He and Perry were discussing the matter in one of their first disputes. She suspected that by tomorrow at this time, it would just be Jane, Jenny, Kincaid, and whichever one of the men was left to care for Kincaid's personal needs.

Well, and the prisoner, and his guards. She'd thought through all the possibilities and realized that their presence might complicate her plans.

She stepped back and clasped her hands at her waist. "Are you going to move Sir Richard?" she asked.

"He's gravely injured," Shaldon said. "There may be no point if he dies before standing trial. And we'd have to keep him safe on the road."

"Keep him safe?"

"From his accomplices who won't want him to talk."

"He might recover. And then what? You'll be in London, and he'll be here, trying to escape."

Shaldon raised an eyebrow. "You wouldn't mind subjecting him to the cruelty of a bumpy road, Lady Jane?"

Guilt gnawed at her. That bumpy road would be dreadful for a wounded man. Still, she needed Sir Richard's pack of guards gone if she had any hope of leaving without interference.

She handed Kincaid his napkin. "You're dribbling on the sheet."

Kincaid grunted again and mopped at the stains.

"Sir Richard might recover," she said again, "And the condition of Lady Perry's neck persuades me that, bumpy roads or smooth, he should travel down to London for a trial. I'll have nothing to do with nursing him."

Kincaid's spoon paused midair. "She makes a fair point."

A frown spread across Shaldon's face. "It's a damnable revenge," he muttered.

The Spy Lord had a conscience?

And so did she, but dammit, she also had a responsibility

to be in London with one thousand pounds. She lifted her chin. "Not revenge, my lord. Justice."

"Bring Fergus MacEwen back from that inn." Kincaid's spoon rattled in the empty crock. "I'll make the arrangements for Sir Richard's transport."

Shaldon looked pointedly at Kincaid.

"Aye," Kincaid said, "Mac's doing good work, but if I know him, he's got himself far too cozy with the innkeeper's girl, all without ferreting out any more details about John Black's operation."

Hearing the ins and outs of these men's seductions was too much. She picked up the tray. "I'll send Ewan up to help you wash."

When the door closed on her, Shaldon pushed away from the wall and loosened his neckcloth. "I'd best go and see to my own packing. Come up to town when you know that wound won't open. You'll be in good hands with Jane."

Kincaid's brows knit together. "She'll bolt."

"Bolt?" Shaldon fiddled with his neck cloth again, considering.

No. Kincaid was wrong. Jane was proper, calm, a rock. "In spite of her help last night, in spite of what happened between...me and Lady Jane, she's not the impetuous sort."

"No?"

The raised eyebrow made his stomach churn again. He pulled the neckcloth off and mopped at his head. The cloth came back stained. Blast it, he was bleeding again.

"Have her look at that," Kincaid said slyly. "Mayhap she'll get impetuous and convince you she'd make you a proper wife. One not so impetuous as to switch out a counterfeit painting for your ransom."

An ache started up in his shoulder. "Enough." Kincaid's experience of women—of one woman—had soured him about matrimony. In any case, he wouldn't allow anyone to speak ill of his dead wife.

Theirs had been an arranged marriage—Felicity had been set to marry his brother the earl, and when *he'd* upped and died she'd settled for the spare, tolerating his refusal to give up his work for the Crown. Felicity had always loved a good flutter, a hell-for-bent ride, and her own way in things, but she'd done right by the estate and the children. He'd been gone much of the time, and when he wasn't, they'd rubbed on well enough together.

The ache crept up and gripped the back of his neck.

But sending the counterfeit painting—he'd never have judged her capable of that.

Still, he had no need for a wife now, placid or otherwise.

It was near dark when Jane left the kitchen, her candle held high, lighting the shadowy servants' staircase. She'd left Jenny and Ewan to see to the men coming in for their dinner. Cup after cup of tea had kept her awake while she bided her time until the house was quiet.

Passing the dining room, she peeked in. A few last rays of late summer sun eked in through the westerly window. The table had been cleared of all but a brace of candles and the white tablecloth, and a few of the fiddleback cherrywood chairs sat pulled back, as if the men had left hurriedly. In the far end of the room, the sideboard loomed in the shadows, two more branches of half-burned candles at the ready. She stepped closer and let out a long breath.

The canvas still lay there.

She scanned the room. Shaldon wasn't lurking here.

Perhaps, after the events of the previous night, he had turned in early.

She tiptoed across the wooden floor to the sideboard, lighting the branch of tapers there.

Someone had removed the painting from its frame and stretchers, leaving it bedraggled, the crimped sides standing up to form a platter of dark canvas with a heart of shimmering light.

Reverently she smoothed out the edges of the ancient canvas and studied it. She had seen a Caravaggio last winter, or rather a copy of one, brought back from Italy by a marquess's son. This work was in much the same style. Two luminous characters, anguished, clothes tattered, eyes raised to heaven, glowed from a well of gloom and shadow. She had been wrong—the work wasn't at all ugly.

This brooding, dramatic, priceless painting should not be a pawn in the conflict between Shaldon and San Sebastian. Making it disappear would be a blessing to everyone.

She would seek Madame La Fanelle's cousin's assistance. Madame had gained Barton's trust; she and her associates and family had withstood Bakeley's rigorous screening before his investment. She could trust them also.

And perhaps theft wasn't required. Perhaps she could just borrow this masterpiece, sell enough copies to pay the debt, and surreptitiously return the original to its owner. She would have to ask Madame's cousin what he thought would be best.

She drew a fingertip along the crease of the canvas where it had been tightened against the wooden stretchers, marveling that such a fragile thing should hold up so well. Along one edge, dark marks, ink perhaps, had bled through from the underside. Lifting the edge and peering closer, she could make out a series of numbers.

Strange.

The work was much smaller than the Caravaggio she'd seen. It was about the size of the small landscape that hung in the bedroom she shared with Lady Perry. She spread her hands wide, taking its measure.

Rolled up, it would fit nicely in the gold-painted rolling pin.

"Where is my daughter?"

Alarm pounded through her. She dropped her hands to her side and froze, eyes shut tight against the flare of panic.

Bloody Shaldon tracked her *everywhere*.

Warmth touched her waist like a bolt from on high, sending hot desire wriggling inside her. Since his turn with the laudanum, Shaldon wouldn't stop touching her.

When this was over, she would think seriously about taking a lover, if she could find some gentleman as appealing as Shaldon who would have her, as old and poor as she was.

She glanced over her shoulder, seeing only his beard-shadowed jaw. "I couldn't resist the temptation." Her voice shook and she eased in a breath. "I've never seen a real masterpiece."

"It is remarkable, I suppose."

Unlike many of his peers, Shaldon didn't collect art. Shaldon House boasted only family portraits and a few paintings of favorite horses and landscapes. His interest lay in collecting and squashing his enemies.

Her heart pounded wildly. If all went right, she would soon be in that number.

"Have you seen Lady Perry, my dear?"

His breath tickled her ear, and the hand at the back of her waist slid a bit further around, bending her to him.

She lifted his hand away and turned to face him.

Dark eyes sparkled in the candlelight, completely unreadable. She rooted her feet resisting the urge to step away, risking the nearness. She could see the pulse in his temple and—

"You are bleeding, Shaldon."

A bead of blood sparkled and threatened to roll down his cheek. His neckcloth was loose and stained red where he must have mopped at his wound. Under the neckcloth, his shirt flapped, more blood coloring the white linen there.

She dug in her pocket for her handkerchief and pressed it to his head. His hand wrapped hers and his gaze softened, setting her insides melting again.

When this was over, she was definitely seeking a lover. Not Shaldon, of course. Not him. She must not fall any further into his enticements.

She drew her hand away and studied the wound. "Sit down, my lord." She nudged him into a chair, pressing the cloth to his head again. "We'll hold this here for a few moments. Do close your eyes."

His lip quirked. "Why?"

"I can see the pulse in your temple pounding. You must take deep breaths and calm yourself."

"Must I?" he asked, lifting a corner of his mouth in a half-smile. "I find that difficult to do when I'm around you, Jane."

But he obliged her by closing his eyes, the half-smile still in place, and she counted out sixty seconds, studying him.

Scrapes and splotches of bruising colored his jaw under the black and gray scruff of his beard. He'd been too beaten up for a comfortable shave. The skin on his knuckles was cracked and still raw. The night before, the dragoon's surgeon had tended to wounds on his chest. The spreading blood on his shirt meant that something was wrong there underneath the white linen.

She pulled her handkerchief away and his eyes flashed open.

"There. The bleeding has stopped."

"Has it? My pulse is still pounding, Jane."

She gritted her teeth. "But there is blood on your shirt and it is spreading. I'll have a look at those injuries."

"Very well." He shrugged an arm out of his coat sleeve, wincing.

"Let me help you." Standing behind him, she wouldn't feel so exposed, or so tempted.

She pulled the coat and waistcoat away while he flung off his neckcloth and pulled out the tails of his shirt. She peered over his shoulder and took in a sharp breath. Blood spotted the shirt in several places.

"You should not have been up moving around so," she said.

"Yes, yes. Help me out of this, Jane."

He raised his arms and she pulled the shirt over his head and gasped.

Fresh bruises and scrapes layered old scars that crisscrossed his back.

The Duque de San Sebastian had done this. She knew it. This she didn't have to ask.

Under all his fine tailoring, he was every bit as broad and as muscled as his henchman lying up in the bed, but Shaldon had suffered more. Those scars explained his drive for vengeance.

She circled around him and dropped to her knees. Every inch of his chest bore bruises and abrasions over more scars. When she raised her eyes, he was watching her.

She tucked a stray lock of hair behind her ear and tried

to rise, wobbling. His hand shot out and steadied her, his other reached for her waist.

Someone knocked firmly on the door, and Jane jumped back.

Shaldon had left the door ajar. Blast it. Whoever was there had seen them.

CHAPTER FIVE

"Enter," Jane said breathlessly.

The door moved a few inches. "Is there aught else you need tonight?" Jenny's voice came from the other side.

She let out a long breath. "Bring some hot water and clean towels, the salve left by the surgeon, and my sewing kit."

"The surgeon felt stitches weren't needed," Shaldon said.

"Because he's a poor hand with a needle. Or perhaps you wouldn't hold still for him."

"It's true I prefer your doctoring to his."

Her cheeks heated. Before the retching started, no *doctoring* would have taken place between them last night. Shaldon would have had her skirts up and her spinster self under him as soon as he'd reached his bed.

"Are you going to examine me, Jane?" he asked warmly.

"When Jenny returns with the water."

He took her hand in both of his and she gulped in air.

"I must clean off the fresh blood first."

His warm touch crept up her arm, as insidious as his hot

gaze. Kincaid had whispered that this warmth, this seductiveness, was due to the laudanum. Shaldon certainly had never been amorous with her before.

And yet there'd already been whispers about her presence in his home. His children might know little of his reputation, but she'd heard the talk over the years from the first time she met him in Kent, little more than a child herself. She'd been half in love with him herself for an afternoon.

A man this handsome, apart from his wife for so long, a man like this had women whenever and wherever he wished. She might like to be one of those women, but with the Spy Lord, it could never be on her terms. His price would be far too high.

"Your assistance has been invaluable, Jane," he said.

Her breath eased. That had been said with a bit more propriety.

"I'm glad to have been of assistance to Lady Perry." And she could help the girl more—and her own plans. "You asked me to make the journey here to preserve Lady Perry's reputation. However, it appears you've solved that problem by sanctioning her marriage to Mr. Fox. I don't know how much more I can do for a woman of four-and-twenty."

"And?"

"She won't wish to be parted from him, and I don't think it's wise to do so. You should let Fox travel with her."

"And what of your safety when everyone has left?"

"It will only be for a few days."

His mouth firmed. "Would that I could stay here myself and protect you, Jane, but the King is demanding my immediate presence."

"I see." The King's command was not at all surprising. After so many years ruling in his father's stead as regent,

Prinny would have his grand coronation, and an earl, even this earl, disobeyed at his own peril.

Thank heavens for that order. It would get the troublesome Spy Lord out of her way. But she must somehow make sure he left the painting at Gorse Point Cottage. If he took it with him to London, it would be ten times harder for her to steal, especially if she was delayed caring for Kincaid.

"If Fox travels with you, and if Bakeley will see to the Special License, Lady Sirena can arrange for the wedding clothes and a small celebration. You should not delay the wedding."

A frown started between his eyebrows.

"Or, perhaps, Lady Perry and Fox can travel to Cransdall with some of your men and marry there by banns in a few weeks."

His frown deepened. "It may be too dangerous. The men traveling to Cransdall will be carrying the painting."

Her heart slammed into a rapid beat.

He wasn't taking the painting to London. He wasn't leaving it at Gorse Point Cottage. He was sending it to his country home, a place she'd never visited; a place a hundred times more difficult to steal from.

"It's that valuable?"

"To the man who wants it, yes."

He glanced at the painting, and when he turned back to her, there was a light in his eyes that she couldn't decipher.

"Jane. Tell Lady Perpetua that Fox may come with us. Ewan will stay here with you. You'll be safe with him. He's acquitted himself well on other occasions for us. As soon as Kincaid heals enough to travel, you may return and help Lady Sirena with the wedding preparations. I fear she'll *need* your help."

"I assure you, Sirena is capable of arranging a gown and a small—"

"No." He squeezed her hand. "Lady Perpetua and Mr. Fox will marry by regular license at St. George's with absolutely all of the *ton* present and accounted for."

"I see." Poor Perry, and poor Fox. "To delay the wedding —is that wise?"

"The days will pass quickly. He won't change his mind."

She shook her head. "Is there not more possibility of danger for him?"

"He won't have the painting or the prisoner. He'll be safe at Shaldon House."

"Let me speak plainly, my lord. What if Lady Perry is—"

"Jane." He raised her hand to his lips, sending ripples of warmth through her. "I would have liked to have removed her from further temptation of that sort. I would have liked to stay here myself and protect you. But you are right that it will do no good to separate them. Removing the painting and Sir Richard will take away the threats to Gorse Point Cottage as well. You'll be safe here. Though I don't like leaving my women with such slim protection."

His gaze was intense and promised volumes, although of what she couldn't be certain.

Not love. Not fidelity. But, oh, there was desire there. It would only require her surrender.

She wanted to weep. She wanted him to kiss her. She wanted him to sweep her up in his arms and carry her to his bed.

The letter weighed heavily in her pocket, reminding her of her duty. If only the letter was a packet of bank notes.

A muffled clattering below signaled that they would have only a few more moments.

. . .

Blast it, he finally had this woman alone again, and the servants would come back and interrupt them. Would that he could stay on with her here and send everyone else away.

She lifted the corners of her lips in a taut version of a smile. "My lord, it must be said that I am in no way your woman."

Not yet, perhaps, but soon.

"Let us say then that your safety here is of great import to me, because I hold you in high esteem, my dear."

Her breasts rose on a sharp breath. "When will the painting be transported to Cransdall?" she asked.

And why that question?

But, of course, she was worried the Duque or his men would attempt to seize it here.

"And Sir Richard? Will he be here much longer?"

Both the painting and the prisoner were dangers. "One of the MacEwens will take the painting, the other will escort Sir Richard. They'll leave the day after next, after…"

He'd forgotten. "Fox can't travel with us tomorrow. He's to stretch and reframe the painting."

Her eyes widened and her mouth dropped open, and then she quickly recovered her composure. "Why not transport it rolled? Though I suppose that might damage the paint even more."

The matter-of-factness of her tone sent a thread of wariness through him. He blinked it away. That was his suspicious nature—an old habit. He could trust Jane. "Yes, stretching will preserve the finish."

"Well, then, you forget, I've been pinching my genteel farthings for years. Don't let the task keep an affianced couple apart. Fox may leave with you on the morrow. I'm perfectly capable of preparing and packaging the painting for transport."

"Are you, indeed?"

He let a long moment pass turning over her words and her now cheerful demeanor. His old habits had kept him safe these many years.

Steps clattered up the stairs growing louder and nearer. They had few moments left and he had more to say.

A blush crept up her still-smooth cheeks. When she returned to London, when they'd got past the coronation, then he could recommence his seduction. He must not rush her. And he must set things straight between them now.

"Jane, about last night...my actions...I *should* apologize—"

"You were drugged."

The blush had flamed into anger, not at all the reaction he'd been after.

"Kincaid explained your behavior to me. The laudanum spoke, and you were not responsible for your actions."

Blasted Kincaid.

"No. A gentleman would—"

"A *lady* would understand." She tugged her hand away. "And I do."

"Here we are, my lady." The maid arrived with a tray, and Ewan clomped in behind her with two buckets of steaming water.

Jane's sharp look pained him. "We'll say no more on that subject, my lord. Now, let's have a closer look at those wounds."

THE NEXT MORNING, JANE LINGERED IN THE PARLOR shamelessly eavesdropping.

Shaldon himself had delayed the planned dawn departure for one last meeting with the MacEwens and Kincaid in the dining room. Their voices carried through the open door. Boyd MacEwen was to take the painting to Cransdall, his instructions straightforward and consistent with what she'd expected.

She'd removed the canvas from the dining room the night before, with the excuse that she had to consult Fox about preparing it. With luck, Boyd had never seen it and wouldn't open the package once sealed.

They'd begun to discuss Sir Richard's transport when Perry descended from the bedchamber. Jane held a finger to her lips and led the younger lady down to the kitchen. Fergus hadn't yet arrived for this meeting, but the plan was for him to leave at the same time as his cousin, that much she'd heard. She'd like to linger and hear the rest, but Perry would wonder why.

"Eavesdropping, were you, Jane?" she whispered, smiling. "Anything interesting?"

"Not at all."

"Well, I cannot blame you. It's the only way to know what Father is up to." Perry greeted Jenny who was packing a hamper for the travelers. Dressed in an old travel gown, Perry could have been another maid visiting the kitchen to bid farewell to the kitchen staff. "It's a wonder there's any food left with all these men about," she said.

"'Struth," Jenny said.

Jane peeked in the basket. "Some bread, some berries, some cheese, and I'm adding some hardboiled eggs. You won't starve."

"What about you two?"

Jenny sent her a sidewise glance and squelched a smile. "We'll be all right, my lady."

"We'll go into town and buy food," Jane said.

"Did Father leave you money?"

"He told us the merchants would honor his credit," Jenny said.

Perry reached into her reticule and pulled out a handful of coins and battered notes. "You must take these. I would not blame you if you left Kincaid to his own devices and slipped away. There's enough here for travel and inns." She frowned. "Though I suppose arriving at Shaldon House in defiance of Father's wishes might be difficult. We shall have to find lodgings for you."

Jane's heart beat a bit faster. "Are you sure?"

"Yes. Into your pocket the money must go, before Father comes down and starts asking questions. You may pay me back later. Or not."

As Jane swept the money away and pocketed it, the door crashed open and two large men sauntered in from the stable yard, one wearing dark coats, the other in uniform.

Lady Perry turned on them. "And where have you been, Fergus MacEwen?" she asked.

Jane recognized the dark-haired Scotsman as one of Kincaid's trusted men. Now she could put a name to the face.

"Off twisting the innkeeper's girl's arm, he was," said the other man, a dragoon Jane hadn't seen before.

Jane's gaze shot to Perry's haughty look and then Jenny's red face. The dragoon hadn't recognized Lord Shaldon's daughter. He didn't know he was in the presence of two ladies, but the lout shouldn't talk that way in front of any woman, not even a kitchen maid.

"Hold your tongue." MacEwen sent the dragoon a tense look.

Jenny had turned away, gripping a knife, her back stiff.

"Are you hungry, Mr. MacEwen?" Jane asked.

"Hungry?" the dragoon asked. "He's been feeding on tinder morsels, haven't you, man? I saw you and the wench—"

Perry gasped. "Are you drunk, man?"

"Drunk?" The dragoon blinked, his mouth firming and opening again.

"Leave it." MacEwen glared at the man, shot Jenny a quick look, and then turned his gaze on Lady Perry. "I apologize, my lady. Your father sent me to speak to Kincaid."

The dragoon's head jerked up, his mouth dropped open, and he made a hasty retreat out through the kitchen door.

Under Lady Perry's disdainful stare, blood rose in MacEwen's cheeks.

"They're in the dining room waiting for you," Jane said.

Perry patted Jenny's shoulder.

"The wretch," Perry said. "What does Father want with him?"

Jane took up a towel and began drying the freshly boiled eggs. "MacEwen will be escorting Sir Richard to London tomorrow." She would have to consult a map to make sure they avoided him.

"Let's have a cup of tea," Perry said. "Or perhaps, Jenny, you would like a spot of brandy."

Jenny's head moved side to side. "You need to be off, my lady."

Perry sighed. "It may not be true what the other fool said."

"It is," Jenny said. "I overheard him in the yard yapping about it."

Perry turned the girl around to face her and gripped her shoulders. "Remember what I said. I dragged you to

Yorkshire. No matter what happens, no matter your troubles, I will always help you, and so will Fox."

Jenny pressed her lips together. "Naught happened, I promise you. At least, naught that would cause trouble in a few months' time."

"You'll stay away from him."

"Yes."

"And his cousin. He's lurking about also."

"The cousin is leaving tomorrow for Cransdall," Jane said. "He and two other men are taking the painting."

"Three men?" Jenny asked. "It's that valuable?"

Perry's eyes lit. "Yes. And I learned something else. Father got the painting years ago from a privateer, none other than Captain Kingsley. And—Jenny, you are sworn to secrecy on this—there's a treasure map on it. Well, at least the coordinates to lost treasure. A fortune in Spanish gold, stolen and hidden somewhere in the West Indies."

Jane's breath quickened and she plopped onto a chair. The numbers written on the canvas—no wonder they'd removed it from the frame.

If word got out about the possibility of treasure, it might fetch far more money than any other ragged masterpiece, enough to pay off a young man's debt and give a spinster the freedom to live independently in some semblance of style. And it would make all the men missing it squirm to get it back.

Fox came through the kitchen door to retrieve his promised bride. Shaldon soon followed, his distant and hurried farewell leaving a hollow place in her heart.

If she was lucky, she would never see him again. If she succeeded, if he came after her, the heat in his eyes would not be lust but the same sort of fury he felt toward the Duque.

She would risk it, dammit.

Soon enough, the clatter of wheels and departing horses subsided, and she and the maid were alone.

"Jenny," she said. "I believe tomorrow is a good day to take the cart for supplies."

The girl looked up, pink-faced. "I'll gather my things tonight and be ready, my lady. I'm going with you."

CHAPTER SIX

*T*he rickety cart passed the last low cottage. Next to her on the cart's narrow bench seat, Jenny let out a long breath.

"We've made it through the village," she said.

It had been a near thing. The men carrying the painting had left at dawn, and the others a bit later. They'd waited a full hour after Sir Richard's departure to leave. Then they'd waited some more until the young groom, Ewan, had taken some much-needed rest. It had been another hour before they could quietly hitch up the plodder to the cart.

Back at Gorse Point Cottage, a pot of soup sat on the sideboard next to a note from Jane saying they'd gone off to buy bread, and that wasn't a lie.

In the village, they discovered Fergus MacEwen had dawdled at the inn—for the prisoner's comfort, the ostler had said. He and his men and Sir Richard had left the town only minutes before Jane and Jenny arrived.

Forced to delay so they wouldn't catch up with MacEwen, they'd chatted over their purchases of bread and cold meat and headed south, giving the excuse that they were off to buy fresh eggs from the aunt of a local man, Davy, who'd helped them capture Sir Richard.

That message *was* a lie. Eggs would simply rattle and break. Jane would drive on past the small freehold outside of town.

When they rounded a bend in the lane, her heart sank. Pip, the young son of Davy, and Davy's cousin Edie, stood in the middle of the road.

Jane pulled up the horse and crossed her fingers. Edie had also helped them rescue Lord Shaldon. The girl had once been employed as a maid for Sir Richard. She'd drawn a map of his manor and gone with them to help gain the trust of the squire's remaining household staff. If they asked for her help now, she might not share the news.

But one thing was certain—in the main, the locals knew how to keep secrets.

"Good morning," Jane said.

Edie scowled up at them. She wasn't the most congenial of young women. "If you're trying to catch up with the others, you won't have far to go. You'll hear the squire bellowing all down the road."

"Serves him right," Pip said.

His cousin nodded.

Who could reprimand the boy? Sir Richard had deserved all he'd got.

"With any luck he'll survive to stand trial," Jane said. And with any luck, they could trail behind Sir Richard and his escort until the men reached the London road. She would have to find another route to a coaching inn. Once she and Jenny boarded a coach, MacEwen wouldn't go after them, not with Sir Richard to keep track of. Kincaid might send Ewan, but they ought to be able to dodge one gangly young groom.

And if not? She'd packed the bottle of laudanum and some powders into her case.

Pip turned and waved excitedly. "Da, the lady is here."

Her heart sank lower. Pip's father, Davy, appeared and greeted them. He was a small man, worn down by worry and drink, and she'd never even learned his surname.

Today he appeared to be sober.

"They've sent the lady off to London in this rickety old cart," Pip said.

Davy blinked. Edie's eyes narrowed.

"No…" Jane's breath caught while she searched for words, conscious of the plainness of her dress, the battered cart, and their black valises packed into the back. Her only item of luxury was the Kashmiri shawl wrapped around her shoulders.

"You have chores to finish, Pip. Edie, take him along home."

The young woman latched onto the boy's arm and steered him off the road, under a branch and onto a path that was almost hidden.

"My lady," Davy said, "it's a stout horse you have there but he won't take you all the way to London, nor that cart over these roads."

Heart battering in her chest, she managed a smile. "Of course not. We're not going that far." Not in this cart, nor with this horse.

He rubbed at his chin. "The next coaching inn be some ways south. And I reckon your man might stop there with the squire for the night."

"We'll be fine, I assure you—"

"Begging your pardon, my lady, but the other lady wasn't fine traveling that road to Scarborough."

Lady Perry had been captured on the road some nights ago.

"He's right," Jenny whispered.

"I know as Sir Richard has been caught, but who's to say there aren't more of his crew as might pop up and two ladies on the road—"

"And you think we should turn back," she said, "but we are only going—"

"No, my lady. Not saying that. Only saying, there might be another way."

"Another way."

"What way?" Jenny asked. "Her ladyship doesn't need any trouble."

Davy's lips firmed. "My boy was saved by the other lady."

Lady Perry *had* saved Pip, but just barely.

His gaze was steady and sober. "I can repay a good deed without causing trouble."

Jane let out a breath. "All right," she said. "How?"

Davy came around and clambered into the back of the cart. "Go up the lane a piece and I'll tell you where to turn."

KINCAID RUBBED AT THE BANDAGE WRAPPING HIS CHEST. THE damn thing was beginning to itch in places, a good sign of healing.

And he was fair starving again, another good sign.

The one thing this cottage lacked was a way to call servants. A proper way. He'd bellow out his caretaker's name if she was anything less than a proper lady.

Riding hard and straight through, Shaldon might reach London on the morrow. Fergus MacEwen, who'd left in the early morn, would have a slower course ferrying an injured man. Fergus's cousin, Boyd, however, should reach Cransdall sooner. The painting would go into the vault there for safekeeping while the Earl laid his trap for the Duque.

Blast it. He had to get out of this bed. He pushed back the sheet and sat up, and pain seared him.

Damn. Damn, damn, damn.

He managed to swing his legs over the side and reach for a shirt. At least they'd put him to bed in his breeches.

Downstairs, the kitchen was silent, the hearth embers buried.

A pot sat on the sideboard, the lid tight. A note propped nearby said the women had gone into town to buy bread. And how long ago had that been?

He looked around, trying to sense what was missing. He'd not spent much time in this room after his injury.

The colorful rolling pins caught his eye. Empty spaces outlined by soot showed where two had been removed.

Kincaid's rump hit a chair as he plopped down. Shaldon ought to have listened to him.

Lady Jane was gone, bolted, and the girl with her.

How the hell had the groom, Ewan, let them go? He'd best have got himself up and gone after them. With luck, the boy would catch up with them before they'd had a chance to reach a coaching inn.

And he'd best get his own self dressed and be on his way.

KINCAID MET UP WITH EWAN ON THE ROAD TO THE VILLAGE. The boy's mount was lathered.

He himself was afoot, he was, blast it. He hadn't dared to try to saddle the one horse left behind in the stable.

"Well?" he bellowed.

Ewan's face paled, making his freckles stand up and

shiver. "They passed through the village not long after Fergus. I rode south as far as Fergus's party. No one has seen them."

"Or they're not talking. Take me up then." He pointed at a rock that would do as a mounting block, then gritted his teeth as his stitches pulled, hauling himself up behind the boy.

"Your mount will need a good rest, and we both need to eat. We'll leave tomorrow. We know where they're going."

"I can change mounts and—"

"No."

"But, the lady alone...and her maid—"

"No."

The boy was drawn to the maid, but if ever there was a lass who could protect herself and her lady, that one was it. Not to mention that Lady Jane had depths they'd all overlooked. "They'll stumble across Fergus MacEwen soon enough, and he'll wrap them up and cart them along with him to London."

LATE THE NEXT MORNING JANE AND JENNY QUEUED UP FOR the balding and chubby agent who was taking money and issuing tickets.

When it was their turn, he gave Jane a friendly nod. "And here we are: the lady in the red shawl."

A woman of a height and age similar to her own turned. "Oh my, it is lovely, and I dare say a perfect weight for the summer. I've been admiring it so. How I wish I had something like that for the coach trip to Nottingham. Visiting my daughter and new grandson there, I am."

Jane smiled as the woman moved away.

Next to her, Jenny glanced around the bustling hall, her

gaze more assessing than fearful. They'd spent a comfortable enough night, sharing a bed in a prosperous fisherman's cottage, thanks to Davy who'd sailed them by skiff to Scarborough and lodged them with kind friends of his. This morning, they'd made their way afoot to this inn in East Sandgate.

The place was busy, and yet, it wasn't likely that Ewan or any other of Kincaid's men would find them here. Coaches left from this inn, but it was also a link to the London packet, and as luck would have it, the regular boat was leaving within hours.

"So, madam," the agent said, "tickets for you and your, er,…"

"Daughter." Jane pulled out the bank notes. This transportation was very dear indeed, but Shaldon's men, if they looked for her, would expect her to be traveling by coach.

Jenny eyed the money changing hands, biting her lip. They went to take a seat in the busy tap room. "If I were to take the stagecoach, would he give you back my fare for the packet, my lady?"

Jane shushed her. "You must call me Mother. And I wouldn't put a maid, much less my own daughter, on a coach to travel alone."

Jenny's gaze went to the door and she slipped down in her chair. After a moment, her frown eased and she shook her head. "A tall, red-haired boy. He looked for a moment like Ewan, but it weren't him." She bit her lip and frowned. "It might be better to pack away your shawl."

Her shawl. Of course.

She quickly removed it and folded it onto her lap.

"It's pretty," Jenny said, "but it does stand out."

"Yes, you're right." A chill draft blew in through the open door and snaked around her, making her shiver.

"Was it a gift?" Jenny asked.

She nodded. "From my brother. He gave it to me not long before he died."

Her brother, Lord Amsden, had arrived at the family estate in Kent, gift in hand. The French had recently landed a small invasion in Wales that'd been quickly snuffed out. Alarmed, Father had felt the need to spend time at his coastal property, and he'd sent for his heir to join him.

Amsden was wild, always on the outs with Father. He'd arrived and presented Jane with the shawl, laughing heartily that he'd won it in a card game from a nabob newly returned from India. She didn't care that he hadn't purchased it especially for her. She'd loved her brother.

Amsden had also brought along a friend, Reginald Dempsey.

A coach horn blew and she roused herself, fingering the fine wool. The inn room stirred with a bustle of people rising. She spotted the woman bound for Nottingham.

She was boarding the London coach.

Jane caught up with her before she reached the door and handed her the folded shawl. "For your journey," she said.

"But—"

"I insist," Jane said. "It would bring me great pleasure to think of you holding the new babe with this warming both of you. My, er, late husband was a merchant, and I have others similar to this at home."

"Hurry along now," the innkeeper said. "Leaving in moments."

The woman quickly pulled off the knitted brown wool draping her. "Take this then, with my great thanks. Made it myself I did." She curtsied. "And may your pretty daughter give you many happy grandbabes."

Jane swallowed tears and slipped back into the corner with Jenny.

"I'm sorry," Jenny whispered.

Her insides shook. She pulled the brown knit close. It smelled faintly of rosewater.

"Don't be. It's just as well."

She was embarking on a criminal enterprise. It was time to let go of the sentimentalities of the past.

She stroked the brown shawl, examining the stitches. "The work here is very good. We've made a good bargain. It was cold on the water yesterday. This will be much warmer."

Jenny nodded, her face a pasty oval. The girl had reluctantly boarded Davy's skiff, only because the other option was to stay behind. And now they'd be sailing on a larger ship.

"I've been back and forth to Ireland many times with no trouble," Jane said. "And I've heard that the Channel packets are very clean and comfortable." She patted Jenny's hand. "And if your stomach gets queasy, I'll show you some tricks that will help."

Jenny sighed. "How long 'til we reach London?"

"Days. How many will depend on the wind." And she wasn't sure if it would be better to arrive in London earlier or later. By now, Kincaid knew she had left, and knowing him, he was up and out and on her trail. And perhaps he'd tear his wound open again and be laid up again for a while.

Though she didn't wish the man any ill, truly she didn't.

"They'll look for the cart and the horse," Jenny said.

"And not find it for several more days." Davy had promised that.

"They'll be checking the inns," Jenny said, "but maybe not the docks."

"With luck. And then we must find a place to stay when we arrive in London." Thanks to Perry, they had enough money for a few nights' lodging.

Jenny nodded. "I've been thinking on that and I know just the place."

THE NONDESCRIPT TERRACED HOUSE AT NUMBER 18, Gerrard Street, stood shoulder to shoulder with its neighbors, all looking glum on this rainy afternoon. As planned, Jane and Jenny continued on past to the junction, where they turned.

Proceeding too far would put them on a street perhaps less than safe for a respectable mother and her daughter walking alone, traveling cases in hand. They soon turned into a narrow mews and found their way through the house's back gate to the servants' entrance.

How far she had fallen. Though they'd had exceptionally fair winds and made good speed, she'd still had much time for thinking in the days and nights aboard the packet boat. Her chances of being tried as a thief and transported—or worse, hanged—grew exponentially with each passing day.

She squared her shoulders. She must be grateful and just as wily as the man she'd robbed. The Earl of Shaldon had not found out about her theft yet. Or if he had, he was biding his time before pouncing.

Jenny pounded the door rather loudly. "Mr. Lewis is hard of hearing," she explained.

An older man in simple workman's attire appeared and squinted at them.

"Who is it, then?" asked a small woman peering around him, the lace on her mob cap fluttering.

"Jenny?" The man's face broke into a gap-toothed smile. "Well, if it ain't our Jenny. And I thought you were lady's maid to a countess."

"I am, but I'm serving Lady Jane Montfort here for a time."

"That is true," Jane said. "May we enter, Mr. Lewis?"

He pulled the door wide and scooped up their bags one-handed, while the older lady ushered them into the kitchen.

Mr. Lewis introduced her as his wife. "Our little Jenny has done well for herself," he told his wife, "though I'm wondering why she's appeared on our doorstep with her lady and is entering through the kitchen door."

This came with another smile that eased Jane's nerves. Jenny had promised she'd be welcomed at this house, which belonged to Lady Steven Hackwell. Jane was acquainted with the warmhearted lady, an eccentric, a bluestocking, and a not entirely acceptable member of the *ton*. Before her marriage, the former Annabelle Harris had filled this home with children like Jenny.

Her own presence here, if known, would likely bring more gossip down on Lady Hackwell. She had business to see to, and an important call to make, but she mustn't stay long.

"We're but seeking a few night's shelter," Jane said. "With the crush of the coronation, the inns and hotels are filled. I'm acquainted with Lady Hackwell and will send her a note tonight. Jenny suggested the lady wouldn't mind our presence. I do have a friend I may lodge with when she returns to town in a few days."

There. That was the story they'd prepared, and one the Lewises readily accepted.

They ushered her to a bedchamber and served her a warm meal on a dinner tray, while Jenny helped her out of her dress and into one of Lady Hackwell's old dressing gowns, and brought her ink and paper.

Later, Jenny slipped out to see to the letters to Lady Hackwell, Jane's dear friend, Barton, and Madame La Fanelle.

When the girl had left, Jane picked up the two rolling pins she'd taken from the Gorse Point Cottage kitchen and examined them. Both were undamaged. The striped tube she set aside as a gift for Mrs. Lewis. She placed the gold painted one carefully on the fireplace mantle, bracing it with a heavy candle holder, and then went to the chair by the dead fireplace and waited.

SHALDON GAZED OUT OF THE WINDOW OF THE DARK COACH, watching a stream of porters and maids and ladies entering and leaving the busy modiste's shop.

"You were up all last night," Kincaid said. "Let me take this watch, and you get some rest."

It had been little more than twenty-four hours since he'd received confirmation of Lady Jane's disappearance, just as his daughter and her new husband were departing St. George's for their wedding breakfast.

He'd left that celebration early.

Where had Lady Jane Montfort gone?

"What of the Duque's movements?" he asked.

"The usual. Balls, gaming hells, and brothels. Nothing out of the ordinary."

Fear gnawed in his stomach. He'd sent men to all of Jane's London acquaintances, as well as to the home of her only relative, her cousin, Lord Cheswick. No one had seen Lady Jane or the maid, Jenny, who'd also gone missing.

Where the devil was Jane?

She'd stirred his suspicions and he'd ignored them. He'd misjudged her.

The temptation to touch her, to test her reactions, to seduce her if she would let him, had overwhelmed him. He'd pushed her too hard. He'd frightened her away. She'd bolted, as Kincaid had predicted, and now she might be in danger.

"That man of the Duque's, the Major, arrived back in town," Kincaid said. "Might have been him behind the attack on Boyd. Follow him, and we'll find the painting."

Boyd MacEwen and his men escorting the painting to Cransdall had been set upon on the road; one had been killed, the rest wounded. The attackers—and the painting—had vanished.

Had the Duque's man taken Jane also?

He couldn't think about the painting with Jane missing. In any case, no doubt, the Duque had taken it.

"Remember that Lady Jane was seen on the London stage line," Kincaid said, reading his thoughts.

"A sighting based on a shawl."

"A very distinctive and valuable shawl. Ewan says it was her. By now, she's arrived here. I've men checking all the inns and her last lodgings, but never you fear; your lady will find her way to her old friend, Barton, soon enough."

Kincaid's smug certainty grated. "Or perhaps she'll seek out her new friend, Madame La Fanelle." He glanced at Kincaid and caught a flash of anger in his longtime acquaintance's face. "And there's the lovely Madame as we speak, boarding a hackney with an armful of dresses. She's a wealthy tradeswoman now and as attractive as when you first met her in France. Perhaps you should follow *her*."

"I'd rather take men and comb every furlong of the London road." Kincaid growled. "No point in following Marie. Unless a few gold crowns dropped into her bag, she'd not rouse herself for the intrigue. Barton's the one that will lead us to your missing lady. Providing the lady and maid are not lying beside that London road somewhere."

Shaldon gritted his teeth against a rising panic. "She's here." He had to believe it. It had to be true. "What the hell did I miss?"

"You were distracted by sudden lust."

The lust hadn't been sudden—it had crept up on him, from the moment he'd seen her at the Hackwells' ball earlier that year.

Hell, he'd noticed her before, many years ago when he'd visited her father in Kent. She'd been a bright, beautiful, cheerful young girl with flattering stars in her eyes, so of course he'd noticed her, even though he'd been too old, too married, and a father to boot.

When next they'd met at the Hackwells', her beauty had matured, her cheerfulness had sobered, and her brightness had clouded to an opaque mystery that intrigued him. She was no longer young, but also no longer too young for him.

She'd lived quietly after her father's death and only returned fully to London society in the last year. What had happened to her in those intervening years?

The only one likely to know was her cousin, Cheswick.

He must speak to the man himself.

CHAPTER SEVEN

*S*haldon paced the drawing room of the Earl of Cheswick's small townhouse on an older street of Mayfair. Faded but comfortable furnishings filled a room strewn with evidence of family life, including books, games, and an embroidery bag. Cheswick was known to be reclusive and bookish. He and his lady were seldom seen at society events.

After an impolitely long interval, the porter returned and escorted him up to another room, the home's library. Books crammed every shelf and nook. Cheswick rose from behind a desk piled with newsprints and journals and came around to shake hands.

A dour-faced man of medium height with a physique gone to middle-aged pudginess, Cheswick had been on course for an academic life at Oxford when Jane's father dropped dead shortly after his son's murder. Cheswick had wanted his title even less than Shaldon had desired his own. But here they were.

"I assume you have come to inquire about Lady Jane,"

Cheswick said. "I'm sorry she's inconvenienced you. Have you uncovered her whereabouts?"

A slow burn churned within him. Cheswick's polite concern was more about Shaldon's discomfort, not the lady's absence.

"I have not," he said. "And it occurred to me that you might be able to give me more insight as to where to start looking."

Cheswick blinked. A sheen of dampness formed on his brow.

Technically, Cheswick's was the older title. He could tell Shaldon to go to the devil if he wished. But he was not, as Shaldon had suspected, a man inclined to direct confrontation.

Cheswick crossed his leg. "Lady Jane is the independent sort."

"Is that why you never insisted she marry?"

He pulled a face. "One does not insist much with Jane."

That was a trait he hadn't seen in the lady.

"Is that why you didn't marry her yourself? When her father died, everyone thought a marriage between the two of you would be likely."

Cheswick's lips pressed together, his distaste evident.

Shaldon's stomach clenched but he kept his fists unfurled, waiting.

"She was too young. We didn't suit. How will this topic help you to find her whereabouts?"

"I should like to determine her state of mind. I'm concerned for her."

"She has done this sort of thing before. She will turn up, perhaps in Ireland. She has a cottage there and visits it from time to time."

"She has property?"

Cheswick waved a hand. "It's a house and garden only. No tenants attached and much in need of repairs, I fear. I transferred it to her name when she reached her majority. In the last few years, she's spent little time there and neglected its upkeep. It wouldn't surprise me, though, if she traveled there."

With no clothing and no word to her friends?

"She disappeared for some time after her father's death. Is that where she went?"

Cheswick tapped a finger on the chair arm. "Yes."

Some part of that answer had been a lie.

"She was grieving precipitously." Cheswick's eyes narrowed. "Her brother's death was especially painful. You will recall his unexpected passing, since you were present."

Since you were present.

A trickle of perspiration rolled down Shaldon's back, under his shirt and coats. *Since the death was your fault.* The unspoken words batted around in his head, starting an ache that reached to his neck.

Jane had gone to Ireland after her father's death. What had she done there? The country was always awash in rebellion and betrayal. Had she been involved?

What had he missed about Jane?

"Her activities there were of no concern to the Crown, if that is what you were wondering," Cheswick said.

He reached for calm, composing his face back into a careful mask. "It was said that she'd been left a comfortable income, yet she lives very frugally."

Cheswick's jaw firmed. "A blunt enough comment, Shaldon, and let me be equally blunt. I've not embezzled, stolen, or otherwise squandered my cousin's inheritance. If you'd like to know why she lives frugally, you must ask her."

"When I find her."

Cheswick pushed to his feet. "Now, I have an engagement to see to. I shall send word to you immediately if Jane contacts me."

"Please do so, and let me know where she is."

Cheswick's lips firmed. "I will, if she allows it."

Thunderstruck, Shaldon rose and followed the man.

If she allows it. Cheswick would preserve Lady Jane's secrets—*was* keeping her secrets, he was sure of it.

They must put a man to watch Cheswick also.

IT WAS NEARING MIDNIGHT WHEN JENNY SCRATCHED AT LADY Jane's bedchamber door. She opened it and ushered in the dark-haired Madame Marie La Fanelle. Petite and still beautiful, Madame had supposedly escaped France as a young woman just in time to dodge the guillotine.

Madame clutched her hands and examined Jane from head to toe. "Safe travels?" she asked.

"Yes."

The French woman's gaze ran over Jane's flannel dressing gown again and she smiled. "I should have brought night clothes as well as the dresses I have made up for you."

Jane shook her head. She would have to pay Madame later for those dresses commissioned for the coronation and never worn. She hoped the debt would keep. "Thank you for coming. Barton surely would have been followed."

"She is hard at work, as are all of the girls." She kissed her fingers and flung them out. "*Merci*, King George, from the bottom of my heart."

Jane laughed along with her. Away from her regular customers, Madame was good company.

Upon their first meeting, Madame and Barton had come to an immediate mutual respect. Individually, each woman was an excellent designer, but together they were exceptional.

"I should like to come and help you," Jane said. "I ply a good needle."

"*Non.*" Madame shook her head. "I prefer you out in the highest society wearing our gowns.

"I fear I may not be able to afford them."

"My dear Lady Jane, whether you pay us or not, we shall be offended if you let anyone else dress you. It is a pity you missed the coronation and the grandest fêtes, but the parties have not ended, and your new gowns are still hanging in the shop. Barton cried when you were not here to wear them."

Jane laughed at the picture of Barton crying. Her former lady's maid had a mountain of good sense and very little sentimentality.

"I cannot pay you for the gowns, unless..." She eased in a breath. "I would ask for your help, Madame."

"In what way?"

"Once you mentioned an elderly cousin who handled... antiquities and art."

Madame's dark gaze became hooded, her manner more careful. "And?"

"And you said that he'd been primarily an artist before escaping the Terror."

Madame nodded.

"Will he help me? Privately? I shall pay a handsome commission, once I am able."

"And if you are not able?"

If she were not able, she would be dead, or locked in the Tower.

She must not think about that. Either result would mean she'd failed the most important person in her life.

"I know there are very few sure things in this life, but I believe I have found one."

Madame waited.

"I've come into possession of a valuable painting. I should like to find a buyer for it."

"Quietly, I surmise."

Jane nodded, her pulse quickening. Yes, she would sell the painting quietly, just as quietly as she had slid into this criminal pursuit.

"You must know, my cousin, Guignard, is also skilled in copying such art."

"Yes, and that is a consideration also. The work has been copied once already, but I know I have the genuine article." She went to the mantel and retrieved the gold-painted tube. "I'm afraid it has suffered much abuse."

Two days later

SHALDON HAD JUST BUTTERED HIS TOAST AND STARTED ON the pile of that morning's post, when Kincaid burst into the breakfast room.

Lady Sirena raised her blonde head from the scandal sheet she was perusing and frowned. "Kincaid, should you be up and about with that wound not yet properly healed? Oh, do sit down, and our man will make you a plate."

He and Kincaid had both been up half the night, moving from one likely haunt to another, and there was still no word of Jane. His few hours of rest had not been enough, and he took the paper Kincaid thrust at him with a meaningful glare. He had one just like it in his stack of morning newssheets.

"'Tis a fact that his lordship takes all the papers," Sirena said. "And reads them also."

"Yes, my lady." Kincaid seated himself and began digging into the food placed in front of him by the footman.

Sirena laughed. "Well, and 'tis also a fact that I've a busy morning ahead." She pushed away from the table and beckoned the footman. "Come along and close the breakfast room door so his lordship and Mr. Kincaid may talk without interference."

Her cheek dimpled around her grin as the door closed. She'd no doubt be sending a servant out for another copy of the paper Kincaid had presented for her private review.

"'Tis news that you have, I suppose," Shaldon said, copying his Irish daughter-in-law.

Kincaid rolled his eyes.

"An incipient insurrection? A spurious diplomat? A—"

"A rare painting for sale."

He flipped to the advertisements, his pulse accelerating.

And there it was.

A rare seventeenth-century painting by a Spanish artist living in New Spain. *Lost and recently found. Lovingly restored. Private bids only. Write for information.*

The address given was the newssheet's.

He tapped the paper. The Duque would never offer the painting for sale. So, it had not, as they'd feared, been the Duque's men on that road. Then who?

And what of Lady Jane? Dread slithered through him. Perhaps she *was* lying dead between London and Yorkshire, while he'd been running after the long train of the King's coronation robe.

"Any more news of Jane?"

Kincaid shook his head. "The only sighting has been that one of Ewan's."

He'd talked to Ewan himself. The description he gave was convincing, but what the devil was she doing traveling alone by coach?

"What word on the maid?" he asked. "Did she return to Charles and Graciela?"

"No answer to that yet. They're on their way to London. Perhaps the maid will arrive with them."

"And Barton?"

Kincaid chewed a mouthful of food and swallowed. "I sent a man in to talk to her. Swears neither she nor La Fanelle know aught of Jane's whereabouts. She hasn't left that shop except to make a delivery or two, with none to Lady Jane."

Shaldon took a sip of his coffee. It had gone tepid.

"Perhaps she's there at the shop, upstairs in the living quarters. Perhaps she slipped in without us seeing her." He set down the cup. "Go in and have a look."

"Marie will stick a knife in me again."

"Wait until she's gone out and talk to Barton yourself."

"And you think she'll not lie to me too?" Kincaid scoffed. "Why not search for the painting there, since that's also gone missing."

Unease threaded through Shaldon. Jane had sent Fox off promising to prepare the painting for transport herself.

He shook it off. She wouldn't have—couldn't have—hired men to attack his men. She didn't have a mercenary bone in her body. Nothing her cousin said about her independence could change his mind about that.

"Might Cheswick be right, and she's run off to Ireland?"

"Not without her clothing and personal effects. Let's start again—if Lady Jane was to go to ground in London, where would she hide?"

And why? He couldn't seem to shake the question, or the

obvious answer. He'd pawed her. He'd teased her about marrying a man she found distasteful. He'd ordered her to stay in Yorkshire and miss a once in a lifetime occasion she'd been looking forward to.

She loathed him.

"We shouldn't ignore Cheswick's speculation about Ireland," Kincaid said.

Cheswick had implied that Shaldon bore some of the blame in her brother's death. Did Jane feel that way also? She must.

What else had he missed about her?

"No. Ewan saw her on a London coach." He rubbed at his jaw. "Might she have taken a ship from here to the Continent?"

Kincaid pushed back his plate and stood, wincing. "After I visit the newspaper office, I'll check at the docks."

"Send a man. Go to the modiste's shop first."

"Better I send a man to see Marie."

"It's been too many years for Marie to hold a grudge."

Kincaid turned a reproachful look on him.

He sighed. Of course, he was wrong. He'd been settling old grudges for the last few years. A woman could be just as vengeful.

"You don't know Marie as well as I do."

That was true. Kincaid's romance with La Fanelle had been years ago in France. The enmity Kincaid felt toward her was still fresh though.

"Don't over-tax your wound," he said.

Kincaid grunted and left.

A few minutes later, Bakeley joined him, the footman slipping in behind him to pour coffee.

His heir was, as usual, perfectly groomed and attired,

looking fresher than he had since Shaldon's return from Yorkshire.

"A late morning," Shaldon said.

"I slept."

The King had tapped him for ceremonial duties, and he and Sirena had organized a grand wedding and breakfast for Lady Perry and Fox. He'd done well, this second son of his. He would make a better Lord Shaldon than he himself had done.

"What are you about today?" Shaldon asked. "Spending time with your lady?"

"I'm off to look at a horse."

"Is Lady Sirena going with you?" Bakeley's wife was the daughter of an Irish earl, the family impoverished by horse-breeding and her father's penchant for drink. She was as passionate as her husband about horses.

"No, though I did invite her. She informed me she was spending the morning at Lady Hackwell's with Paulette and also Barton, who's bringing over her latest sketches."

A buzzing started in his ears. Lady Sirena would not turn down a chance to look at a horse, except for something of importance, which would not include sketches of gowns. And his eldest son's wife, Paulette, was not known as a leader of the *ton's* fashion scene, nor was Lady Hackwell. Both ladies, however, were close to the missing maid, Jenny. Barton had been Lady Jane's maid before going into business with Madame La Fanelle. And Sirena had lived with Jane as a companion before marrying Bakeley and taking Jenny as her own maid for a time.

"How is Barton finding the time?" he asked. "I've been watching the shop. It's full of patrons, with porters running willy-nilly delivering packages. Your millinery business has done well."

Bakeley laughed. "If only all my investments were so profitable. Speaking of that, Father, have you decided about a post for Penderbrook yet?"

Quentin Penderbrook, his son Charles's friend, was in dire need of an income.

"I'm asking," Bakeley said, "because my steward in Kent is wanting to retire. I considered letting Penderbrook have a trial."

"In spite of his gambling debts?"

Bakeley paused in cutting a large piece of ham. "Charley said it and he's right—there's something off about those debts. That Payne-Elsdon fellow has bought up all of Penderbrook's vowels."

Payne-Eldon had been a major in the King's army, serving in Spain. His reputation was sordid even without his association with the Duque de San Sebastian.

"I know we promised Charley we'd look into a position for Penderbrook," Bakeley said, "But if he's swimming in the Duque's murky waters, he may need more than money."

Shaldon rose and passed the newspapers to Bakeley. "The one on the top has a most interesting advertisement for a painting. Don't toss it out."

He sent the footman to order his carriage while he went for his hat.

CHAPTER EIGHT

*J*ane held tightly onto Mr. Lewis's arm as he escorted her and Jenny through the Hackwell House mews to the residence's back entrance.

She'd risen early and dressed in her plain traveling gown, an unadorned drab, the better to pass inconspicuously through town. She'd been preparing for the most important visit of her life, when this summons to Hackwell House had arrived.

If Lady Hackwell insisted on this meeting, there must be boundaries to her benevolence.

At the garden door, Lady Hackwell's warm greeting eased the knotting in her stomach, and they climbed up the stairs to a small sitting room.

"My lady." Barton shot up from her seat and came to greet her, with Lady Sirena joining in, and Mrs. Gibson reaching for Jenny.

A tea tray littered with empty cups sat atop the round table, and Barton's large portfolio lay open next to it.

"I'm sorry we're late. We decided to walk." It wasn't far, and she needed to conserve her coins.

"Next time I'll send a carriage," Lady Hackwell said.

"Or I will," Sirena said.

"Better I should," Paulette Gibson said. "The Gibsons are not so grand. Bink and I, being mere commoners, generally find it easier to elude Lord Shaldon than the rest of you."

Her stomach fluttered. So, they all knew she was avoiding the Earl.

"You are so kind." Jane forced a smile. If they knew the whole truth about her flight from him, they might not be so willing to help.

A maid appeared and refreshed the table, and they all seated themselves.

She was grateful for the few moments to gather her thoughts. She must have a care what she said. Other than Barton, none of the women present, not even Jenny, knew the extent of her duplicity.

Barton brought her a cup and a plate, worry clouding her eyes.

"Well," Sirena said, "What's afoot, Lady Jane? What has Shaldon got up to with you?"

The mouthful of biscuit stuck in her throat. She took a sip of tea and set her cup aside.

"This has nothing to do with Lord Shaldon," she said.

"Everything has something to do with Lord Shaldon," Paulette said. "Or rather, he is so often behind tweaking our strings, he has something to do with everything."

She had heard the story—Shaldon had arranged the marriage between Paulette and his eldest, Bink Gibson, managing to capture a traitorous marquess in the process.

Lady Hackwell's lips formed a thin, disapproving line. "Has this to do with Mr. Morton?" she asked finally.

Jane squeezed her eyes closed a moment. "No." Once a

tidbit of news surfaced, there was no possibility of keeping a secret in the *ton*.

Unless one was dealing with the criminal element. She prayed she could count on Madame and her cousin, at least for a time.

"I refused Mr. Morton's offer. And I assured Lord Shaldon that not even his endorsement of the match would convince me to say yes."

"*What?*" Lady Sirena rose and began to pace, her gown framing the babe growing inside her. "I shall tell Bakeley to...no, I shall have a word with Shaldon myself. To think of him attempting to force an ancient roué on a handsome woman like you, still in her prime. Why, no wonder you didn't return to Shaldon House."

"No, Sirena. No, that's not why I didn't return to Shaldon House. Not entirely. I..." She bit her lip and fought for a breath. "Perhaps I just feel that I've...I've gone a bit mad."

Sirena frowned. "The letter from your solicitor—"

"A private matter." She stood and took the younger woman's hand. "Oh, do forgive me. You've been so kind." She spun away, alarmed to feel tears welling.

"Besides providing you inconspicuous shelter," Lady Hackwell asked, "how may we help?"

"We dearly wish to help," Sirena said.

A thousand pounds would do.

She wouldn't ask it though. "I thank you," she said finally. "I only ask a few more days' lodging."

"And then?" Lady Hackwell asked. "Will you go to your cousin, Cheswick?"

"He has also been very good to me, but no. I'm considering...I'm considering going abroad."

"Back to Ireland?" Sirena asked.

"Perhaps."

"Or Paris," Sirena said. "Barton, you should go with her and bring back the latest Paris fashion plates when you return."

"I'll be happy to go also, my lady." Jenny moved from her post near the window.

"I...I haven't decided."

How far would she need to run from the Earl of Shaldon?

"We shall revisit this in a few days," Lady Hackwell said, "but meanwhile you must feel free to use my carriage. Have Mr. Lewis send for it when needed."

"Do you mean to go out in society at all, my lady?" Barton asked. "If so, we have your new gowns—"

"No, Barton." She shook her head. "For now, I must see to some business, and I would appreciate you keeping my presence in town confidential." Especially where Shaldon was concerned.

"I wonder, would our husbands keep the secret?" Sirena said.

"Lord Hackwell will," his lady said, "if I choose to tell it to him."

"After what we've all been through with Shaldon?" Paulette asked. "Good heavens, Sirena and I were almost killed by the men he was chasing. Our husbands would keep mum. However, they would each try to run to your rescue, Lady Jane, whether you wished for their help or not."

She swallowed back more moisture. To have men who would care so much was a great blessing. Also, a huge annoyance if one didn't want to be rescued.

And she was quite sure neither the ladies nor their

husbands would want to help her if they knew the truth of her plan.

"Thank you. And I do beg your pardon, but I must be off to attend to another matter."

Jenny turned to the door. "I'll get our—"

"No, Jenny. I won't require your company today."

Lady Hackwell rose. "You will go in the Hackwell carriage. Do not worry, we shall have you exit quietly through the mews."

Lady Hackwell was wonderfully kind, but she could also be firm, and in truth, Jane didn't want to run into any of her acquaintances while walking down Piccadilly.

She gave instructions to the coachman, accepted the footman's hand up, and sank into the plush cushioning. As they pulled into the busy street, she hastily closed the shade.

Panic rising, she took deep breaths and fought to still her heart. There must be no tears this day, no matter the outcome.

By the time the coach stopped at the Burlington Arcade, she had found her courage again. She instructed the groom to wait for her and walked determinedly through the Arcade and out of the back way onto Burlington Gardens.

The gentleman she must visit had a bed-and-sitting in a private home near here. Thank heavens he was not at the Albany, where one of the other men in residence might recognize her.

She pulled the sides of the poke bonnet forward and marched on. It was time to officially meet her son.

THREE LADIES EXITED HACKWELL HOUSE TOGETHER AND climbed into the escutcheoned Shaldon coach. Shaldon recognized his two daughters-in-law, Lady Sirena and Paulette. The other lady was the maid-turned-modiste, Barton. They'd arrived together, and they were leaving together.

He'd gone down another blind alley.

A red head appeared at the coach window.

"My Lord, she's leaving the mews in the Hackwell coach," Ewan said.

"Get in."

The boy balked.

"Get in, I said. Riding outside, you're far too conspicuous." He shouted an order to the driver and tugged the boy in as they pulled away. "You're sure?"

"Yes, my lord." Color surged in the boy's cheeks, making them almost as crimson as his hair.

"You'd best be right."

"Yes, my lord."

"You are the one, are you not, who spotted her at an inn on the road. How did you not catch up with her then?"

They'd been over this before, but he always found that hearing a story a second time provided more clarity.

"The lady's coach had stopped for a few minutes and was leaving again in all haste, and I'd just arrived at the inn. I spotted her getting in—it was her all right, all wrapped up in her red shawl, but my horse was completely fagged and the ostler had no fresh mounts. When I finally did catch up to the coach at a later stop, I learned that the lady had left the coach somewheres in between. No one could say exactly where, or where she might have been traveling to from there."

An unmarked burgundy-colored coach pulled out of the mews, distracting him. He caught a quick glimpse of a woman inside before the shade came down.

"That's her," Ewan said.

Leaning back, he tried to dampen a rising excitement, contemplating the best way to confront her. What the devil was she about, running away like that, with nary a word to the people who cared for her?

When he'd met her as a young girl in Kent, she'd been a year or two away from her come-out. But old enough to be allowed at table for the quiet country dinners hosted by her father, the Earl of Cheswick.

Shaldon had been a guest at some of those dinners. He'd barged his way into the last one, his real purpose being to meet with Reginald Dempsey, who'd joined Jane's brother, Lord Amsden, in the country. Jane had blushed prettily around Dempsey, who'd shown her a brotherly affection. That she had a *tendre* for Dempsey was to be expected—he was a strapping young man bursting with pride about his work for the Crown and his private engagement to a rich merchant's daughter.

That marriage had never occurred.

The coach moved lazily through building traffic, easily keeping a distance from the quarry.

"I lost a man once in Kent," he mused, watching the crowds on the street.

"My lord?" the boy prompted.

"Damnable thing. Damnable results. I lost him, and he circled around and killed two of my men."

One of his men and the man's friend, who'd insisted on coming along. Lady Jane's brother had died that day, along with Dempsey.

Hackwell's coach wound its way to the Burlington Arcade and discharged its passenger. She took no more than a few steps before Hackwell's footman caught up with her.

Jane turned on the man with more intensity than he'd ever seen her display.

Ewan was already opening the door, but Shaldon stayed him.

"I'll go," he told the boy.

"But, my lord…"

He climbed out of the coach. "You lost her once."

He hadn't lost a mark since that disaster in Kent. He wouldn't lose her today.

As she left her footman and blended into the crowd, Shaldon pulled down the brim of his hat and followed.

She wasn't here to shop. She simply kept moving, brisk and sure, all the way through the arcade and onto the street beyond.

JANE SLIPPED UP THE EMPTY STAIRCASE QUIETLY AND KNOCKED on a dark paneled door, waiting. Light filtered in through a skylight above, highlighting the fading paint, nicked moldings, and worn stair runners.

The door opened and the starched servant who answered flashed her an astonished look.

She handed him her card and put a hand on the door. "I'm here to see Mr. Penderbrook."

He cast a worried look over his shoulder.

She slid one sturdy half-boot forward. "Is he presentable?"

"He is…" He glanced at the card. "He is at breakfast, my, er, lady."

Pasting on a smile, she pushed the door open and brushed past him.

Quentin Penderbrook was a young man of four-and-twenty, but the look on his face when he saw her was that of an astonished toddler. Wonder and shame warred in her, as it had each time she'd seen him.

But she must proceed. She was tired of lies and secrets, and he, above all people, deserved the truth.

If she could bring herself to it, he also deserved a good dressing-down.

He shot to his feet and fumbled with the ties of his banyan. A bachelor, he'd just risen from his bed and strolled into the next room to dine, much as she'd done in the rooms she'd taken last year when she and Sirena arrived in London.

"My lady." The servant hovered nearby.

She turned on him. "I must speak with Mr. Penderbrook in private." She handed him a coin, and he looked at it, perplexed.

Not very bright, this servant.

"Run out to the corner and buy Mr. Penderbrook whichever newspaper he is missing."

When Penderbrook nodded, his man left.

"My lady, I'll just go and finish dressing."

His trousers peeked out below his dressing gown and above his house slippers.

"No. Please be seated."

Fumbling again with his banyan, he looked around. "Will you join me? Have a, er, coffee?"

She nodded and began to pace. He picked up the serving pot and put it down again. Only one cup and saucer graced the table.

"I'm quite fine," she said.

He remained standing.

He was a gentleman, with handsome looks, and handsome manners. He wouldn't sit unless she did.

She pulled over a chair and sat, and so did he, perching on the very edge of his seat.

"Are you well, my lady?" he asked. "I'd heard a rumor you were...you had not returned from Yorkshire."

She shook her head. "I should, perhaps, have done this differently. But I am here, and I will speak."

His eyes went impossibly wider and he sat up straighter. "No, my lady, let me call you a hackney and escort you home. You are too far above me...I am a mere vicar's ward."

Laughter bubbled in her along with tears. She swallowed both back and struggled to remain dignified, as if that were possible in this circumstance.

"You misunderstand," she said, "and I am so very s-sorry..." She cleared her throat. "I should have spoken to you earlier, after we met at Mr. Charles Everly's wedding." She had sat beside Penderbrook in the carriage that day, wanting ever so much to embrace him.

She should have spoken to him earlier, or...not at all. She could still leave.

No—it was too late. She couldn't leave Quentin thinking she was a middle-aged lady looking at him with amorous intent. The very thought made her skin crawl.

She straightened her shoulders. "Mr. Walker, the vicar who brought you up, were he and his wife good to you?"

He blinked.

"You called them uncle and aunt, did you not?"

Now a sharp look crossed his face, but he quickly schooled it. "They were both very kind."

That relieved a burden on her heart. "They never remonstrated you about your...about your parentage?"

He blinked. "What?" A red tint bloomed on his cheeks. "They were very kind."

"You've grown into a fine gentleman."

"Thanks to my uncle and aunt. They provided me everything."

She nodded. "Everything. Good."

"What is this about?"

The reports to her through the years had been accurate. Quentin's childhood had been a happy one. "They took excellent care of you. I'm so very glad."

"My lady..." His voice rising, he stood, and so did she. "My lady, let me escort you home. You are distressed, and—"

"Penderbrook," she said, "Quentin. I am...I am your mother."

She flinched. Her voice had risen also. There was no telling if these walls were thick, or if the other tenants might have heard. Color swept up his neck and his hands fisted.

If she'd wished for a happy ending, this wouldn't be it.

There was relief in the telling, yet life seemed to bleed from her, and she moved sluggishly nearer the door.

Still, she must finish what she came here to do. Reluctantly, she turned back to him. "I am aware of your gambling debt."

That knowledge caused his high color to drain. His lips went to purple, genuinely worrying her.

"Perhaps you should sit, dear boy."

"My lady, you should leave now," he said, voice quaking.

"I want you to know, I mean to continue to help you."

"I don't need your help."

She winced at the shouted words. "I'm sorry. I've bungled this. If you ever wish to know about your f-family, you have only to contact me. Otherwise, my solicitor will be in touch when I've secured the funds you need."

"I know my family, my lady. And I don't need your help.

I have prospects and my income from…" He paused and his mouth dropped open.

From me.

"My dear boy." She turned away before he could see the tears threatening. "Farewell."

She pulled open the door and came face to face with Shaldon.

CHAPTER NINE

*P*anic tore through her. *Dear God*, how much had he heard of what she realized now was a very loud conversation?

She caught her breath. "My lord."

"Lady Jane," he said, all affability. His face was…softer, kinder.

He'd heard.

Her face heated. Her fingers curled into fists.

She'd kept her secret for over two decades, and now the nosiest, most irritating, most interfering man in all of England, a man who'd almost seduced her, knew the truth. Oh, he wouldn't share it, that she knew, but he'd find a way to use it against her all the same.

Damn and blast it all. She'd sell his damned painting and not think twice about it.

She slid past him. A hand wrapped her arm, the touch firm.

"You are most welcome back at Shaldon House."

She gritted her teeth. "Thank you, Shaldon."

"Where are you staying?"

"With friends."

"I fear your failure to return to us was due to my conduct."

Heat pounded through her again. "I always hasten to remember what they say about visitors and fish kept for too long." She shook her arm free and escaped down the stairs.

A tall red-haired boy lingered outside near the street. Could her afternoon get any worse?

When he fell in behind her, she rounded on him.

"Go away, Ewan," she said.

"I'm sorry, my lady, I can't."

She stepped out into the street and he pulled her back, in time to save her from a speeding phaeton.

Pulse pounding, she drew in a breath. She didn't want to die this day, not really.

"Thank you, Ewan. You may escort me as far as Burlington Arcade. My carriage is waiting there."

He offered his arm, and still quaking inside, she took it. It was a solid arm for one so young, and she wondered if Ewan treated his own mother this kindly. She suspected he did. He was likely respectful, and considerate and kind, and very likely he loved his mother.

Quentin Penderbrook despised his, and what could she expect?

Perhaps she should have stayed in Ireland and let him dig his way out of his own gambling debts. He was a grown man and didn't need a phantom mother coddling him.

But, oh, the hurt she'd seen on his face—*she'd* caused that.

Tears welled and tipped over her lashes and she battled them back.

They found the Hackwell carriage and Ewan helped her in.

"Don't follow me," she said.

The boy gave her a direct look, his hazel eyes clear above all his freckles. "My lady, I lost you once. If I lose you again, Lord Shaldon will sack me."

"And if he does, you can go back to the Gibsons."

"And then Mr. Gibson will sack me. The truth is, we all worried something terrible had happened to you somewhere on that road, you and the maid. Until I saw your shawl and knew you were on your way to London."

The shawl. Jenny had been so right. Thank God the girl had been bold enough to speak up.

"Is the maid—"

"With me? Yes. I'm sorry to have caused you worry." She signaled the coachman and they pulled away. With the state of the traffic, Ewan would have no trouble following her. She must send a warning to Jenny, Mr. Lewis, and his wife to not answer the door.

A FEW MINUTES EARLIER...

SHALDON LINGERED A MOMENT ON THE SIDEWALK GETTING his bearings. He knew the residence Lady Jane had slipped into. It was, in fact, his afternoon destination. And what the devil was she doing visiting a single young man here?

Jealousy pricked at him, but he shook it off. He knew of women Jane's age and older who took a favorite footman or other young buck to bed. Jane wouldn't.

Would she? There was passion in the lady, bottled up for years. Would she go after Penderbrook?

The boy passed himself off as an orphan, raised in the care of a country vicar he called uncle. He might well be a wealthy man's by-blow well-concealed, but he doubted his son Charles would have stayed friends with the boy if he was hiring himself out to older ladies as some sort of *cicisbeo*.

And if not that, what would he have to do with Lady Jane?

A servant rushed out of the door and down the street, just as Ewan appeared.

"I stayed back, my lord," Ewan said. "She didn't see me. And you might need me."

He sighed. "Disobedient, but in this case your instincts might be correct. Wait here. If she appears without me, follow her."

He crept up the staircase. Most of the rooms were quiet, but muffled voices from an upper story were a beacon. The walls and doors of this narrow home were thin.

When he reached Penderbrook's door he paused and pressed an ear to the panel.

"My lady, let me escort you home. You are distressed, and—"

"Penderbrook. Quentin. I am your mother."

Shaldon's breath caught as it almost never did, his mind careening in dizzying calculations. Was it possible? Penderbrook was...younger than Charles, yes, but Lady Jane was still not yet forty.

But she'd gone off to Ireland after her cousin inherited, and her grief might not have been the only reason for the journey.

He'd been too busy to pay attention.

Blast it all to hell, he hadn't wanted to think about Jane then. Thoughts of her and her brother always came with a hefty dose of guilt, a useless emotion, one he didn't indulge in if he could help it.

And guilty he was, and how she must hate him.

"I am aware of your gambling debt."

A worrisome pause ensued. Might she need his assistance? Penderbrook was a gentleman, but young men did not like to have their faults scrutinized, especially by women.

"Perhaps you should sit, dear boy," she said.

"My lady, you should leave now."

Shaldon put his hand on the latch.

"I want you to know, I mean to continue to help you."

The voices grew louder. He stepped back from the door.

"I don't need your help."

"I'm sorry. I've bungled this. If you ever wish to know about your f-family, you have only to contact me. Otherwise, my solicitor will be in touch when I've secured the funds you need."

And how was she to do that?

"I know my family, my lady. And I don't need your help. I have prospects and my income from…"

Penderbrook's income had been from Jane.

That truth was a sharp blade to *him*. Penderbrook must be reeling.

He'd missed it—he who prided himself on seeing the secret failings and hidden desires of everyone around him. Jane had borne a child. She'd used her inheritance to support an illegitimate son, all the while living like a poor relation.

Because her brother had died.

"My dear boy. Farewell."

He'd barely registered the sadness in her voice when the door opened.

Astonishment lit her face. All the color drained and then surged back up her neck and into her cheeks.

And he *knew*. He knew how she meant to secure the funds.

She slid past him.

"Jane." He touched her arm, so fragile and yet so strong. "You are most welcome back at Shaldon House."

"Thank you, Shaldon."

"Where are you staying?"

"With friends."

Guilt rose and clogged his breathing. Botched missions that ruined the lives of innocents were all too often a part of this business. That particular botched mission had been his failure, and this woman had suffered for it.

He cleared his throat. "I fear your failure to return to us was due to my conduct."

Color flooded her again, turning her cheeks a brighter shade of red. "I always hasten to remember what they say about visitors and fish kept for too long."

It was a lie, and they needed to be done with lies, he and Jane.

He watched her hasten down the stairs. Ewan would be there to watch over her, and this time the boy would not lose her.

He stepped into the rooms and closed the door.

"M-my lord." The young man in front of him gave a ludicrous bow, given the state of his undress, and then swiped a hand through his hair.

"Quite a morning for you, isn't it?" Shaldon placed his hat on a stack of papers. "You've made a hash of that last call. Let's see if you can do better with this one. Fetch another cup and—no, on second thought, I think something stronger is in order."

"Brandy?"

He nodded, and the boy went for the bottle and glasses.

He hated the stuff, but they both needed something to stiffen their pride, both of theirs just crushed by a woman.

Penderbrook poured and they clinked glasses and drank.

"Did you...hear, my lord?"

"Yes."

"I didn't...I never suspected. How old...how can it be possible? I'm sorry."

A memory came to him—the Cheswick parlor, Lady Jane looking up adoringly into Reginald Dempsey's face, and Dempsey returning a grin that was...playful, he'd thought then.

Now he knew. That had been lust, satisfied, and damn it all, he hadn't suspected *then*.

"You will have to ask her those details, and you may do so...tomorrow night. There must be some ball, or rout, or some such."

"The Kennerly musicale."

"Good. Were you invited?"

Penderbrook nodded.

"I'll make sure Lady Jane attends."

"How?"

He fixed the young man with a stern gaze. The boy needed hardening. He'd been coddled and pampered by the bookish vicar who'd raised him. He'd been seeking a position in the Foreign Office, but he'd never make a spy or a diplomat. First, he needed to step up and be a man.

For Jane's sake, he would settle the boy's debts, and then he would find Penderbrook another type of post. After the boy made amends with his mother.

"You'll send her a note, asking to speak to her there. Lady Bakeley will ensure she attends."

"Yes, my lord." Penderbrook went to a sideboard and retrieved a sheet of parchment. "Where is she staying?"

"You may send it in my care."

Penderbrook lifted his quill, but Shaldon stayed his hand. "You will write the note before we leave, but first we will talk about your debts to Major Payne-Elsdon. Has the man called you out on them?"

The boy's Adam's apple rippled and a mulish look came over him. "Not yet, my lord. I've...I've been expecting his challenge every day."

"And how did you come to gamble so much with him?"

"I've only wagered with him a couple of times when I... when I was much in my cups. And I'd paid those wagers with the help of my..."

Penderbrook's jaw dropped.

"Your mother."

The boy swiped a hand through his hair, perspiration rising on his brow. "I thought the funds came from my guardian." He colored deeply. "I had no idea."

"And so, if you paid those wagers..." He leveled a hard gaze at the boy.

"The Major has taken up all my other vowels, even from friends who'd assured me they would happily wait."

"How?"

"The moneylender I...er...dealt with was, of course, quite happy to be paid by him. As for my friends, when they've wagered with him and lost, he's accepted my vowels in repayment."

"Has he indeed. Well, sit down, and let's have a reckoning of the debt."

JENNY HEFTED HER BASKET, LETTING HER GAZE SWEEP THE street and the passersby as she headed back to the house on Gerrard Street.

She'd lingered at Hackwell House until Lady Jane's carriage had returned empty. The coachman had dropped Lady Jane at Barton's shop.

Jenny had hurried to join her there. Something was wrong with the lady, something more than just feeling a bit mad—as many women did from month to month, and wasn't Lady Jane still having her courses?

She'd heard of that paunchy old gent's offer of marriage, but she suspected Lady Jane had received plenty of such offers, if not of marriage, then of the other sort, men being men.

It might not be any of her affair, but she was curious, and a bit worried, like one might be about a favorite aunt, if she'd ever had one of those.

At the modiste's shop, she'd found Lady Jane in the thick of it with an oily old Frenchman, who'd put her in mind of a fence she'd once seen in her old life. Their crew had filched a whole set of miniatures and—

At the back gate of the Gerrard street house, a tall gent stepped out of the shadows, halting her train of thought.

CHAPTER TEN

*H*er heart clacked and then settled again. Though perhaps she oughtn't to feel so reassured about this tall gent being his lordship, the Earl of Shaldon. Dressed as he was, he looked much like a street boss she'd known in the Seven Dials.

She curtsied and drew closer—but not too close. Out of arm's reach, she needed to be.

"Jenny," he said.

Well. He hadn't called her *girl* this time.

She held his gaze, probably too boldly for his sort, but never mind. Lady Jane needed her boldness.

His lip quirked ever so slightly. "I'm glad you are safe."

"Thank you, my lord."

"Jenny, I've knocked on the door, and no one will answer."

She let out a breath. It was lucky Mr. Lewis could read. Lady Jane had somehow got wind of Shaldon finding out where she lodged and had sent a note of warning. "Her ladyship's orders. She's not receiving visitors."

"She's not home."

He was certain, was he? He'd probably followed Lady Jane all the way to the dress shop. A laugh gurgled up, and she swallowed it.

The dark gaze drilled into her. "Is she coming back?"

A right wily man was Lord Shaldon. His gaze revealed nothing, not what he thought, not how he felt, not what he knew. He wasn't looking at her like she was a plain servant, or a chit to be swived, or a criminal he could threaten with the law. It was hard to lie to a man like that. "Yes, my lord, as far as I know, she's returning here." Though she supposed that might change if Lady Jane knew Lord Shaldon was lurking.

"Will you let me in? I'll wait in the parlor for her return."

She lifted her chin. He was a powerful lord, and she a mere maid, but she knew her duty. "No, sir. She's...she's having a rough go."

He opened his palm and a coin caught the light. A gold sovereign. The urge to grab it and bite down was powerful.

A sigh escaped her. "Not even for that, my lord." She steeled herself against his gaze, waiting.

"The Service can use a stalwart heart like yours," he said.

MacEwen's boasts about dallying with the inn maid flashed in her memory, and her blood rose. "No thank you, my lord. I could have had that life in the Seven Dials."

"That's not—"

"No." She shook her head. "I've seen your kind of life, and the one I had before, and I'll stick with what I have now. I like regular meals and a roof over my head, and it hasn't been boring. And I know, even if you dismiss me, I'll be able to find honest work."

"Very well." He pocketed the coin and drew out something else. "I promised to deliver this to Lady Jane." He handed her a sealed letter. "Will you place it into her hands?"

"Yes, my lord. That I'll do."

She watched him move down the mews wondering why that had all been so easy.

JANE ARRIVED HOME IN THE LAST OF THE LATE SUMMER twilight and found Jenny and the Lewises waiting for her in the kitchen.

She declined a warmed-over meal, having already dined with Barton and Madame, and Jenny followed her up the stairs to the bedchamber.

"If you'll but help me out of this gown, you can be off. I'm for bed."

"Are you well, my lady?" Jenny asked, unfastening her gown.

"Only fatigued," she lied.

Madame's cousin, Monsieur Guignard, reported that the advertisement placed in the paper had spurred strong interest.

But he'd also heard murmurs, that others had heard of the painting's discovery even before they'd placed the notice. Worse, the substitute painting she'd wrapped for transport to Cransdall, the landscape from the Gorse Point Cottage bedchamber, had disappeared. The men conveying it had been attacked. One of them had died of his wounds.

Moisture clogged her throat. Because of her actions, a man had *died*. Did he have a wife or children who loved him? What was her sorrow about her son's rejection compared to that sort of loss?

But had the murder truly been because of her? The men

were attacked and the package stolen before they'd ever opened it.

Still…she wanted to curl up and weep over this day.

"There now." Jenny had reached the last hook. "Lord Shaldon was here, my lady, asking to be let in."

She tugged out of her sleeves and pulled down her bodice, her head pounding. Running into Shaldon at Quentin's had been a stroke of terrible luck.

He had seen the Hackwell carriage. He had puzzled out Lady Hackwell's ownership of this property.

Ewan had tracked her to the modiste's, of course, and promptly informed his master. Had they seen Guignard at the shop? Shaldon would know who he was—Shaldon knew everything.

She would need to act quickly. She'd instruct Guignard to take the best offer and make the deal, tomorrow if possible.

"I turned him away. He offered me a gold sovereign, the cheeky old codger."

"*Jenny.*" She choked back a laugh. Cheeky the man was, and old she supposed, but he was no codger.

She stepped out of her gown. "I'm glad you didn't take it." She couldn't have faced him again this day. She couldn't face him tomorrow either when he would surely return.

Perhaps Marie knew of another place she could lodge for a few days.

Jenny shrugged. "It might have been painted lead."

Jane turned and took the girl's hand. "Dear Jenny, coming from him, it would have been genuine. But never mind. In a few days, I'll have enough money to give you a gold coin before I leave England. You may even tempt some bounder like Fergus MacEwen to marry you."

Jenny stepped back and put her hands to her hips. "I've

no interest in a faithless man, my lady. And you'll need a maid wherever you go. Lady Perry once said we could live well in France at far less cost."

"Should we run off to Paris together?" The girl's steadfastness cheered her. "Help me out of the rest of this."

Jenny went to work, undoing her stays and dropping the nightgown over her head. This one was a sheer lawn, with soft lace framing the deep rounded neckline and capped sleeves.

"This looks new," Jane said.

"Madame sent this home for you." Jenny smiled. "The nights have been too warm for Lady Hackwell's old woolly nightrails."

Jane held back a sigh. She had yet another debt to Madame. She sat and began removing her stockings. "Go on then. Off to bed with you."

"There's just this, my lady." Jenny reached into her pocket and pulled out a letter, placing it into her hands. "From Lord Shaldon."

She knew Shaldon's writing, and this wasn't his.

When the door closed on Jenny, she poured a glass of sherry and downed it, examining the letter again, unable to determine who'd sent it.

Once Shaldon took hold of a notion, he was relentless. What was he up to now? He would insist on an interview. He would persist until she'd told him everything.

And then, if he didn't see her arrested, he would drop her, just as he'd dropped her father after her brother's death. He'd rushed out of Kent as if nothing had happened, as if she and her father had not had their hearts torn out. Shaldon had been involved, her father had implied, but he wouldn't say how.

Damn the man and his games—this letter could wait for the morning, when he'd launched his next move.

When she'd recovered more courage.

She propped the letter on the mantel next to the china shepherdess, settled onto the armchair near the cold fireplace and began taking down her hair. Long and still thick, it hung almost to her waist. She'd once had dark blonde hair. Now, it was a light brown, and in the light of the lamp, the strands of gray threading through it shimmered like silver. She should cut off a good length of it, but she often felt this was all she had left of her femininity.

On the one full night they'd had together, Reginald had marveled over her unbound hair. She squeezed her eyes shut on that memory.

A mere girl of fourteen—how could he have done what he did? True, she'd been more than willing, a thoughtless puppy seeing men for the first time. She'd even been breathless around Shaldon—who hadn't noticed her at all—until Reginald had appeared.

She poured another sherry and drank it down. The past was over. The son Reginald had left her with *still* required her help. She needed to sleep for just a few hours and move quickly tomorrow.

She rubbed her eyes and raked her fingers through her tangles. A stiff brushing was just what she needed.

The dressing table stood behind an ebony-framed screen painted with fading cupids and wreathes. In the shadowed corner, she groped for the brush.

A rustle of cloth sent chills through her, freezing her breath.

Her hand found the brush and she clutched it, lifting it high, ready to strike. Around her, the air filled with scents—

horse, leather, and a subtle cologne, the sort a wealthy man's valet applied to a noble cheek after shaving it.

As her eyes adjusted to the darkness, she backed slowly away watching him rise.

Tall, darkly clad, at home in the night, he loomed over her. She heard her own pulse, heard her tight gasps, smelled her own fear as it turned into rage.

Somehow, she managed a breath.

"Who took your gold sovereign?" she asked.

"JANE," SHALDON SAID.

It was the only word that would come. Her hair swirled around her in a riot of silky waves, and with the light behind her, the diaphanous nightgown made her look nakedly lush.

His body's response was instantaneous and gratifying.

By God, she was beautiful, and by the way she was strangling that brush, she was also infuriated.

He didn't care. Heat poured from her in lilac waves, sending her scent to addle his brain more, to drown him.

When had he last had a woman he'd truly wanted?

There'd been Addy, his son Bink's mother, and Felicity, his wife. Both had betrayed him for their personal causes. For Addy, it'd been the Irish rebellion; for Felicity her love of fine things.

And it was a certainty, Jane had stolen the painting. More hot blood rushed to his groin.

She'd stolen out of loyalty, not betrayal. She'd stolen to help her child fathered by Reginald Dempsey, the man whose death had weighed on his conscience for twenty-odd years.

She had good cause to steal from him.

And he wanted her desperately. The madness of it made him want to laugh, another thing he hadn't done in far too long.

The drugging he'd suffered had blown the lid off the simmering pot of desire he'd become since he'd spotted Jane entering the Hackwell ballroom last winter with Lady Sirena. Bakeley hadn't been the only Everly pole-axed by a lady that night.

He gently loosened her grip on the brush. "Come."

She went, stiff, vibrating with anger held in while he seated her on the hassock, taking the armchair behind her.

"You have lovely hair." *Riotous, wild, glowing.*

All that passion restrained, for so many years. What had Jenny said? She was having a rough go. She'd had a rough go for too long. He would take care of her now.

He plied the brush lightly, again and again, lifting the thick mane from her stiff back, stopping to work the tangles free with his fingers, gently loosening knots.

Slowly, her breath evened out and the high color drained from her neck. Her shoulders turned creamy again under the lace of her gown, her breasts probably also—by God, he wanted another look at her breasts, unbound by stays and bodices.

Her sigh, when it came, sent his heart pounding higher. She'd signaled resignation, not pleasure, but he'd soon enough change that.

Not that Jane would make it easy. How could he have discounted her spark and her strength?

"No one took your gold coin," she said, her voice cracking. "You broke into the house on your own."

To get to Jane, he would have managed a climb to the upper story, even at his advanced age, but it had been more practical to go in through a door. "I shall recommend the Chubb detector lock to Hackwell. Very hard to pick."

"*You should not be here.*"

"Why not, Jane?"

Her throat moved as she swallowed. "Because…because, I am…finished, Lord Shaldon, with you, with society, with everyone. If that sounds ungrateful, so be it. I am *finished.*"

"Where will you go? To your cousin, Cheswick?"

"No. He is better off without me."

No one was better off without Jane. How had he not seen that before? She added grace and kindness and beauty to every room she entered.

"To Paris, then?"

"Perhaps. Or even farther away. Perhaps the Antipodes."

He would not like to chase her that far.

"You would like Dijon, or the south of France better. The people are more congenial. Paris is not a kind place."

"It is surely kinder than it was thirty years ago."

"Madame Guillotine is not killing earls' daughters, if that's what you mean." He leaned close to her ear. "So, you are going to the Continent to live on the proceeds of the sale of the painting?"

A vein thumped under the porcelain skin of her neck.

He dropped the brush and took both of her shoulders, leaning in, inhaling her clean scent.

The shiver that went through her sent an answering thrill through him.

"You know," she said tightly. "Of course you do."

"I suppose I should be cross with you, but I'm not." Jane's unintentional diversionary tactic had saved the painting from whoever attacked his men on the road. "Dear Jane, will you tell me what happened?"

Her chin dipped. Oh, how he wished he could see her

face, but for now, supporting her was enough. He slid his arms around her, the weight of her soft breasts warming his forearms.

His heart pounded as fiercely as hers, her breasts, by God, her breasts, rose up and down over his arms.

"What part?" she whispered.

He eased her off the hassock onto his knees and then fully onto his lap, turning her sideways to cradle her.

For now, she accepted it, the quake going through her the only evidence of resistance.

"You're cold?" he asked.

She made a scoffing noise. "I'm *angry*. You *shouldn't* be here."

He moved a hand to her head to soothe her and took it away. Jane wasn't a mark to be seduced. He wanted her trust, her agreement.

Through the filmy cloth, her nipples hardened. More blood shot to his groin.

Devil take it—since the laudanum had loosened him, he'd been obsessed with seducing her. And he would. Honorably. And he'd never discard her. Never.

He touched a thumb to the peaked nipple and she gasped, clapping her hand over his.

"What the hell are you doing?"

"Coming to my senses." He set his lips to hers and nibbled.

When she squirmed, he cupped her breast fully.

She jerked away, perspiration sheening her brow, her eyes flashing.

Spirit, and passion, and heat—by God, he must have her.

"Jane," he said. "We'll marry." It was the best solution, the most logical. "Make love with me tonight, and in the morning, I'll apply for a special license and we'll wed in the afternoon."

Heart pounding, she covered her ears.

Had she also been drugged? Shaldon's words set a fever swirling through her, a madness of touch and scent and carnal desires. His, hers—they were both caught up in the insanity.

One hand fondled her breast, with the other he tugged her against his solid strength. And her backside encountered a firmness that sent heat flaming through her.

"Jane?"

Eyes gleaming in the light of the lamp, he waited for her response.

This man was not Shaldon, the managing patriarch, Shaldon, the unemotional spy lord.

She wrestled the hot yearning between her legs.

When this was all over, she would take a lover. Tonight, one of them must be sensible.

"Are you…are you drunk, Shaldon? Has someone fed you another drop of the poppy?"

His low chuckle sent a shiver through her and he whispered a firm, "No."

He leaned in, crushing her breasts to his chest. "I am completely sober," he said.

His lips moved over hers, exploring, nibbling, pressing. He tasted of mint, not brandy, so perhaps he was telling the truth.

She closed her eyes and tried to breathe while he kissed a path along her jaw, his cheek sliding smoothly against hers, his cologne filling her senses.

When he slanted his mouth over hers, her lips parted for

him, heart pounding in a welcoming crush, her body beyond her control.

"Jane," he whispered, and moved back to kissing her cheek, her jaw, her neck, while her pulse raced and she grasped for a thread of reason.

She put a hand to his cheek and realized—he'd shaved for this encounter. He'd planned this seduction.

Nosy, managing, infuriating man.

He kissed her again, tongues tangling. His hand, so large and masculine, stroked down to her backside.

Flailing against his embrace, she tried to stand. He pulled her closer.

"Sh-shaldon." She sucked in a breath. "Come to your senses. I'm a thief, Shaldon."

"I don't care," he mumbled against her neck.

"And a scandal. I bore—"

"A child."

When he lifted his head away, his gaze burned into her. "You were a child, bearing a child. Until today, I never noticed the boy's resemblance to Dempsey."

She caught her breath, reaching back for a memory. She'd forgotten Reginald's face. But of course, Shaldon was right.

Shaldon was always right. Anger burned through her again.

"Once apprised of a fact, you *would* unravel all the strands of a lady's shameful past."

He lifted his head and his gaze pinned her. "A child bearing a child and sacrificing her own life to see to his needs honorably for over twenty years is not shameful. Among the aristocracy, you are one in a million, Jane."

"Oh," she said, the breath whooshing from her. That was

said with a different sort of passion, from a man who knew about secrets, could keep them, would honor them.

He swiped a calloused finger over her cheek. "I am in awe of you," he said, and then he began his assault again.

Her mind ceased to work. Madness welled in her: desire, regret, relief. She should not trust him, could not trust him.

But her body didn't care and she found herself kissing him back.

Her conscience tried to intervene, pushing memories at her. The small cottage in Ireland, her great aunt Mildred, who viewed everything through the lens of the last century's easier moral code, her father's berating lectures and sudden death, her arguments with her cousin.

She'd worn Cheswick down, eventually, and despite his dismay about her wantonness, he'd agreed to her terms for her life.

Cheswick, by some miracle, had left her alone, had kept her secret, had even let her solicitor wonder if the child was his own by-blow. He wasn't a bad man, her cousin, and she'd always been grateful he'd refused to take her on as a wife.

Shaldon pulled away and stroked her cheek, making shushing noises.

She was weeping, blast it.

He pulled a handkerchief from somewhere and dabbed at her face, his other hand locking her close. No man had held her thus, not even Reginald all those years ago. Reginald had looked and touched—her breasts, her buttocks, the place between her legs. Shaldon was looking at *her*, touching *her*.

And for once it seemed he had lifted the shutters to draw her out of her own chaos, to let her see into himself.

She took a good long look.

"We won't do this if you do not wish it, Jane. But I very much want to."

His jaw was smooth under her fingers, and his gaze softened under her touch. She'd desired him, it was true, not just since he'd kissed her.

It was so tiresome being good for so many years. She wasn't that fourteen-year-old girl anymore. If she planned to take a lover, why not start now?

"Yes," she said. "I'll make love with you. But..." She held up her hand. "Not the rest. We will not marry." Marrying Shaldon would be the height of madness.

The air stirred as she floated up, secure in his arms.

"Never doubt that I will marry you."

That last was said stiffly, but when he eased her onto the bed his hot gaze raked over her, sending fresh heat that constricted her breath.

He sent his neck cloth flying, flung off his coats, and sat down to tear off his boots.

In mere moments, he'd removed his shirt, trousers, small clothes and stockings, and stood looming over her.

A scar carved a deep spot in his shoulder, and others crisscrossed his chest and waist, like the ones on his back.

And—her chest squeezed again—the evidence of his desire was clear. She struggled to breathe and let her gaze travel down. The sturdy legs bore their own set of scars, a quite wicked one to a knee, the reason he sometimes limped.

He'd fought many enemies, this man, and been hurt by them.

She opened her arms and he came to her.

CHAPTER ELEVEN

*H*e heard her sharp breaths, felt her quaking, and he reined himself in. He wasn't an unbridled boy. He'd had many lovers.

But Jane? She had little more experience than a virgin just out of the schoolroom. He would gamble his last farthing she hadn't taken a lover after Reginald Dempsey.

Hell, that preening young jackass wouldn't have been a proper lover.

When she rolled and faced him, the bedside lamp highlighted the peaks and valleys under the thin gown.

He smoothed a hand along her hip. "How beautiful you are."

She put a finger to his lips. "No flummery, Shaldon."

She wanted honesty also, this woman who'd kept such a great secret for so many years.

He wanted to know her secrets. He wanted to know *all* of them.

"You've had a difficult few days. How did you elude our men on the road?" That question had been nagging at him.

A smug smile curved her lips. "We traveled by sea."

By *sea?*

He laughed. "You clever girl. Wait until I tell Kincaid. But...Ewan spotted you on the London stage."

"Did he?"

He rubbed at his head. *It was her all right, wearing her red shawl...*

He brushed a lock of hair back from her cheek and raised up on his elbow. "You clever, clever girl. You gave away your shawl. So intelligent. So beautiful."

"Flummery."

"No."

Her sharp breath warmed him as he kissed her, tasting her sherry-scented lips. It was his last cogent thought.

WAVE AFTER WAVE OF SENSATION ROLLED THROUGH HER, igniting more memories. She'd felt this hot desire before, this itchy building pleasure, and pain—the sharp stab of Reginald tearing into her.

And after had come agony. Reginald dead, her brother— who shouldn't have been there—dead.

Her fault. Her brother's death had been her fault.

She'd blamed Shaldon too. He'd been in Kent. He'd been at the gathering where they'd died. He'd come the next morning with the news of their deaths.

It had been Shaldon who'd mentioned Reginald's fiancée.

Kisses, gentle, then demanding, then gentle again, muddled her. Shaldon's hand had found the hem of her nightgown and was inching it up, shocked pleasure streaking through her.

Had Reginald been so gentle? Aunt Mildred had talked of the deep pleasure of coupling. Reginald's careless seduction, her thoughtless capitulation, had brought far more pain than pleasure.

Her chest tightened. Death, betrayal, shame—all the ghosts of her past hounded her, and still she felt pleasure.

The nightgown rolled higher. He leaned in and suckled.

This wasn't the same as before. She wasn't a child. And—she *wanted* him.

She'd robbed him, and he'd caught her out. And he wasn't angry.

They were both candidates for Bedlam.

Only...She squeezed her eyes shut against a flare of panic. Was this his way of getting revenge?

"Jane."

She opened her eyes and there he was, watching her.

"I stole your painting." It needed to be said again. He must understand. "I wrapped up another and sent it north."

"I know."

"I meant...I *mean* to sell it to the highest bidder."

"And give the money to your son."

"Yes, and if this is your way of...of getting revenge—"

"*No*," he roared.

He flopped onto his back and pulled her atop him, skin to skin, hearts pounding together. He pulled the bunched nightgown over her head, tossed it aside, and locked his arms around her.

Gasping for breath, she struggled up onto her elbows and dodged his intent gaze, tracing a finger over a scar. This one was old, lined with puckers where the flesh had been stitched.

Everything he did had a risk and a purpose.

"Not revenge then," she said, her breath tight. "What, besides a tumble, do you really want from me, Shaldon?"

He snaked a hand under her hair and sparked pleasure along her spine, down to her backside, making her quiver.

His hooded gaze raised an alarm in her. Shaldon's will was indomitable. And where pleasure was concerned, she was almost a complete innocent. Since Reginald, she'd never flirted aimlessly—never flirted at all. The cost was too high.

She raised herself on one arm. "I'm not sure this is—oh." Hot sensation snaked through her, rushing heat to her face.

The grin on his face made him look human. "Yes," he said. "That's what I want. Just that reaction."

In a flash, she found herself on her back again. "What I want, Jane, is *you*, well-pleasured." He nibbled at her neck. "What I want is to earn your great heart." A kiss to her jaw followed. "And your enduring loyalty." He pushed a lock of her hair back. "I want all of you, honorably, and forever."

Braced above her, he waited.

Her heart clattered inside her, Aunt Mildred's voice rattling around with it and adding to the noise. *Though it's often enjoyable, men only talk of love when they want a woman to yield.* She'd fallen once, believing sweet words from a rogue who had tricked her and died.

And forever? Shaldon might be hardy, but he was old; old enough to have a son past the age of thirty.

"No one can promise forever, Shaldon."

"The rest of my life is yours, Jane. You have only to say yes."

Why? Why did he want her? He could simply take the painting, now that he—

"You are thinking again." His lips quirked. "Tell me what you're thinking. Just speak…" His hand settled over her breast. "From this great heart."

Her great heart felt ready to burst. She caught her breath. Bed sport between lovers might be prettied up with words, but it was rarely based in anything deeper than lust, Aunt Mildred had said. With a proper and considerate man, a woman would have much enjoyment. Go into the affair with your head on straight and you won't lose your heart. And pay heed to certain other possible consequences.

Consequences like her son, Quentin. "I'm thinking, I would do better to speak from my great head." She placed a hand over his. "Perhaps I am saying yes to tonight."

She sighed and shook her head. Of course, she wanted this, wanted him, had been lusting after him.

"I *am* saying yes, but only to tonight. And I believe you know the consequences that could flow from one night of lovemaking, even at my advanced age?"

His smile grew. "I am willing to risk it, my lady, and perhaps it may persuade you to a second yes."

"The second answer is still no. Though as I recall you made a declaration rather than a request."

"Let me try to convince you."

His grin was so boyish, it made her laugh.

"Very well." She lifted her head and kissed him.

She'd be a reckless gambler again.

He squeezed her breast, and then he was sliding down, kissing her, suckling her, murmuring how beautiful she was through ragged breaths, stroking her hips, her belly, the place between her legs.

Reginald had poked a finger into her there, briefly, before, and then there'd been pain.

Shaldon paused.

"Did I hurt you?" he asked.

"Not yet."

"And I won't. We'll take our time. Trust me, Jane," he said.

Trust Shaldon?

His mouth settled again on her breasts and his hand moved below for long minutes, the sensation exquisite, and she found herself moaning, and then writhing, and then...

Pleasure burst in her, luminous, explosive.

Shaldon was atop her then, and she parted, giving him entrance, gritting her teeth.

He filled her and there was only a satisfying fullness.

They moved together then, in a quick, ferocious drive, the pleasure building and building until she burst again, biting back a cry.

With a fierce groan, he climaxed inside her and collapsed.

TIGHT, TORTURED BREATHS PIERCED HIS CONSCIOUSNESS AND he opened his eyes.

He rolled to the side, pulling her with him. "I beg your pardon," he mumbled. "For crushing you, that is." He'd not ask forgiveness for what they'd just done.

A soft touch smoothed over his shoulder. "So *that* was what Aunt Mildred was talking about."

Fatigue muddled him, as it always did after a tupping. One of the reasons this sort of tactic was better left to a younger man.

But, Jane was not a mission, he reminded himself.

"Mildred?"

He fought the sluggishness of his recovery and listened as she told him about the aunt who had stayed with her and schooled her during her confinement. Some young women would have reacted to such an education after such a scandal by seeking more of the same. But not Jane.

He'd been right about her. She was solid and honest.

Not placid, though. His shaft stirred again. By God, he felt thirty years younger this night.

SHALDON HAD LISTENED TO HER TALE OF HER AUNT, HIS EYES closed, occasionally offering a grunt, until she'd talked him into slumber.

The Spy Lord had fallen asleep in her bed.

She watched him, awed by his vulnerability, and wondered...if she slid from the bed would he wake? If the door to the corridor opened, would he be instantly alert? If she touched him...?

She snuggled closer and one eye opened, and then an arm snaked around her.

He slept, but she could not. This was a night to wonder at. After thirty-nine years of life, she knew what it truly was to make love to a man.

But *marry* Shaldon?

His bed talk...those were just words. Before tonight, she'd only seen his reserved public face, but in fact, he'd sired a bastard and beguiled secrets from countless women in his travels.

No. She couldn't promise to marry him.

Quentin needed her help. She must sell the painting tomorrow. But—what if Shaldon would buy it?

He'd acknowledged her theft and said nothing about buying it. Perhaps he thought a night bringing her pleasure was payment enough. And then what?

Her son needed help. She couldn't rely on the wily Spy Lord.

· · ·

IN THE EARLY DAWN, SHE WOKE ALONE.

Propped on the pillow next to her was a note and the letter Jenny had handed her, the letter she'd put aside last night.

She glanced at the note, squinting in the half light.

I will see you tonight at Lady Kennerly's affair. Do be sure to read your letter. All will be well.

No words of love, no signature, not even an "S". A guarded man was Lord Shaldon. She must remember that.

And she had no plans to attend Lady Kennerly's affair. The man's high-handedness knew no bounds.

The seal on the letter snapped easily, the paper unfolding to reveal a few lines of masculine script.

My dear Lady, I hope you will forgive my rudeness today.

She blinked and looked away, hands shaking and wondered if Shaldon had compelled this letter.

I assure you the harsh words were spoken out of shock and my embarrassment at my circumstances. I should like, if you are willing, to have a private moment with you at Lady Kennerly's musicale tonight. There will be no need for further sacrifice from you, as Lord Shaldon has offered me a position.

Most sincerely, Q.P.

She flung the paper aside, sprang from the bed, and began to pace.

She was twice a fool. It was happening again. Shaldon was recruiting her son into danger, just as he'd done her brother and Reginald.

He'd made love to her only to soften her. Marriage? *Pah.* He wanted her agreement, her compliance.

Oh yes, he'd keep his word and follow through with a marriage—a union destined to be miserable. Shaldon never took half-measures in his managing. He wanted her—and her son—under his thumb.

But why? Why? She had no state secrets. She'd never betrayed England, nor had her son.

She squeezed her eyes on hot tears. In the short time she'd known Quentin, in the few social encounters they'd had since she'd met him, having heard the tales of his gambling and debts, she'd realized he was not suited for Shaldon's type of work. He would be foolish. He would also meet an untimely death.

She must save him.

She hurriedly washed and grabbed a gown. Before she could struggle into her clothing, Jenny appeared.

"You're up, my lady?" Jenny glanced at the bed where both notes lay scattered and the bedsheets and pillows were tumbled. The girl blinked once, and without further comment, went about helping her dress.

"I'm going out tonight." She must make that meeting and convince him to decline Shaldon's offer. "I'll need one of my better gowns. Could you have a note carried to Lady Sirena? She'll find something in my clothes press to send."

"Yes, my lady. Shall we have your whole wardrobe brought here?"

Once her business here was settled, she would leave London quickly, which meant most of her wardrobe would stay behind. Perhaps Madame's seamstresses would like some of her older dresses.

"No. I couldn't possibly keep imposing on Lady Hackwell's hospitality. I'm sure I'm a burden for the Lewises as well. And for you, Jenny."

"No, my lady." Jenny fastened the last hook and tugged Jane's skirts into place. "I'll deliver your note to Shaldon House myself. His lordship knows we're both here, and I doubt he'll clap me in irons. Are you visiting the modiste today? I'll bring whatever gown Lady Sirena chooses to you there."

While the maid went for a paper and quill, Jane twisted her hair into a knot.

CHAPTER TWELVE

*S*haldon's valet had just finished shaving him when Kincaid appeared in his doorway. With one look from Shaldon's old friend, the servant left, closing the door on the two men.

"Charley and Grace arrived in the wee hours," Kincaid said. "You weren't here to receive them, but I was."

Shaldon ignored the dig. "I've been informed." Graciela was anxious to see her father as soon as possible when the man stepped onto English soil.

"And?" Kincaid tossed him the shirt spread out on the bed.

What did you learn last night? Shaldon heard the implied question and dropped the shirt over his head, hiding his annoyance. Kincaid was an insistent bastard at times.

But they had long ago learned to put aside their irritations with each other. "Lady Jane and Jenny are staying at Lady Hackwell's old home on Gerrard Street. She has the painting, or rather she took it and *had* it." Kincaid threw back his head and roared out a laugh that made him wince.

"And did I not say that she would bolt?" Kincaid's gaze

narrowed. "Placid and proper, and you were missing all the night. Have you found a way to take charge of the lady and that painting?"

He tucked his shirt in and reached for his waistcoat. "It wasn't amongst her things when I searched. Did you check La Fanelles's?"

"Did I go into the lioness's den? No. And I don't believe it's there. My best guess is it's with Henri Guignard."

Shaldon frowned. "He's still alive?"

Guignard had been gray-haired some twenty-odd years earlier when he'd slipped out of Paris before Robespierre could nab him.

"Living quietly, plying his trade on the outskirts of London. He was at the shop yesterday. He's Marie's cousin."

His head snapped up. They had worked with Guignard on a few occasions, and Kincaid had never shared the connection to Marie. "Where would he keep it?"

"I don't know." Kincaid rubbed his chin. "He's old, but he's no fool. It will be in a safe place. He'll know the value of it. Besides which, the newspaper had a visit from a mustachioed gent wearing a sword who meets the description of our Major. After that, the paper was broken in to, files tossed. Read today's notices—the publisher is withdrawing from receiving the bids for the painting."

He found a fresh linen cloth and twisted it around his neck. Jane had snatched the painting away not only from him, but from someone else who wanted it desperately. That could only be the Duque.

"Did we have a traitor in our ranks?" he mused. Upon hearing the news that their men carrying the painting to Cransdall had been set upon, he and Kincaid had discussed the question at length. "Have you thought more upon the subject?"

"I've talked to our men here. The painting's discovery was no secret. Word spread quickly and any one of the locals—or even the soldiers—could have passed the news. It was a small step to watch the departures from Gorse Point Cottage and notice three men going north with a package."

Dear God—Jane and the maid might have also been targeted on the road.

"Did the newspaper office have Guignard's name?"

"Possibly, though Henri would be clever enough to give them a false address."

"He may be in danger. La Fanelle—and her partner and seamstresses—might be as well," Shaldon said.

"And Lady Jane. Can you convince her to move back here?"

After tupping her? He'd awoken with renewed desire and a sure conviction that he must leave her bed immediately or else risk spending the whole day there.

She'd been firm in her refusal to wed him. That would change. He would see to it.

He hadn't felt so unsettled about a woman since Bink's mother, when he himself had been a mere pup.

He shook off the sensation. It was his duty to protect Jane, and he'd find a way.

He picked up his coat. "Help me with this." The tight-fitting coats so in vogue were hard to get into without assistance.

Kincaid sighed, but obliged. He had more than once played the role of valet, most recently when they were arranging Paulette and Bink's marriage.

"There you go, your noble lordship," Kincaid said. "I'll snoop around, find out where Henri is lodging, send word to you, and then I'll go face my nemesis and assess the degree of danger to her and her girls. Pray that she doesn't gut me with her sewing shears this time. And where will you be?"

Penderbrook needed a position, and soon. The steward's job was a possibility, but the boy's history of gambling was a concern. A minor bureaucratic spot in the government might be more suitable. "I'll go have a chat with Farnsworth." Farnsworth could make discreet inquiries in Penderbrook's behalf. He might also know more details of Major Payne-Elsdon's connection to the Duque de San Sebastian. If there was time, perhaps he would pay a visit to Lord Hackwell, who might be persuaded to evict his wife's tenant. Though he suspected the strong-willed Lady Hackwell might overrule her husband.

Kincaid left, and Shaldon made his way to the breakfast room. As he arrived, he almost bumped into Lady Sirena hastening out.

He remembered his mission for her—to ensure Lady Jane's presence at the Kennerly musicale.

"A word, Lady Sirena, if you have a moment."

She blinked, glanced down the corridor toward the servant's stairs, and smiled.

"Of course, Father. None of the others have come down for breakfast yet." She dismissed the footman and poured Shaldon a cup of coffee before returning to her own full plate at the table.

She'd left her food to hurry out on some urgent mission. A message from Lady Jane? That would work to his advantage.

His stomach growled, and he filled his own plate.

"I've found Lady Jane," he said.

She sawed at a piece of ham, frowning. "Did you speak to her, my lord?"

"I did."

"I hope you were kind to her."

He swallowed a chuckle. No exclamation of surprise or relief. Perhaps Sirena knew he had followed her to Hackwell House the day before.

"I've asked her to return to Shaldon House." He seated himself and pinned her with a look. "I've proposed that she and I marry."

Her head shot up, cutlery crashed, and a grin bloomed on her face.

"Have you indeed?" Her smile faltered. "I do hope you are sincere. Did she agree?"

"I am, and she did not. I should like your help, Sirena. I should like to make sure she attends the Kennerly musicale tonight."

"I see." She pressed her lips together. "And what do you mean to have happen there?"

"I should only like to spend a pleasant evening in public with her."

"You mean to attend?" A laugh escaped her. "Oh, I do beg your pardon. I'll do my best, I will, providing you remember that Lady Jane has a mind of her own. But if it can be done, I will do it and see that she's properly turned out." She fixed him with a stern gaze. "You don't mean to force her hand in some way, do you?"

"I don't know what you mean."

She rolled her eyes and waved a slim hand. "Drop to your knee during the interval and propose marriage again in front of the *ton*."

He looked down his nose at her and watched the color rise in her cheeks.

She wasn't embarrassed—she was fighting a smirk that bubbled up into a laugh. "Oh, very well. Jenny has come, so I will discuss the matter of a proper gown with her and make all the arrangements. When Gracie wakes, I'll solicit her help also. Or...is it a secret you wish me to keep?"

He would do better wishing for a unicorn to appear in the back garden than to expect her to keep news of this sort from the other ladies.

"If you would but kindly tell Graciela to not share the information, I would appreciate it." Charley's colonial wife could be trusted. The girl was a locked pirate's chest full of secrets, some he suspected, she'd not even shared with her new husband.

"Lady Perry might help also. Though I don't wish to disturb their honeymoon, it *has* been a few days since the wedding. I've been ever so tempted to pay a visit to the townhouse and see how they're faring."

"Best not." The men guarding the honeymoon house reported that the newlyweds had kept mostly to their bedchamber. Another grandchild would be on the way soon. "But do send a note and let them know Charles and Graciela have arrived."

She pushed back her chair. "I'll do that immediately. Jenny can wait. She's probably gossiping and feasting below stairs."

An odd sense of relief filled him. The ladies would not oppose a match between him and Lady Jane, and he doubted his sons would object.

With their help he'd insure Jane's safety, and with his own resources he'd take care of Penderbrook's dilemma and deal with that bastard, the Duque de San Sebastian, and his Major. The Duque's lust for a mere painting would prove a fatal weakness. He was counting on it.

He must pay an immediate visit to Guignard, as soon as he knew the man's direction.

He sent for his coach and made quick work of his

breakfast. As he was pulling on his gloves, the porter handed over a letter that had arrived by messenger.

The handwriting, the scent, the seal, sent a tingle of curiosity through him, but he waited until he was seated against the velvet-upholstered squab to scan the lines of feminine writing.

I would speak to you of your Major. Meet me at half past eleven at the usual place.

He sighed and stowed the note. He would see to the meeting between Lady Jane and her son, but he would have to forgo another night in her bed.

JANE SQUEEZED BETWEEN GRACIELA EVERLY AND LADY Sirena on the gold damask settee in Madame's small parlor and accepted a glass of sherry. Barton took the other free chair, and Madame La Fanelle seated herself behind her elegant writing table.

The afternoon appearance of Shaldon's daughters-in-law was unexpected. Happy though she was to see them, their presence would complicate her business with the little Frenchman she'd been waiting half the day for.

Did they know that Shaldon had visited her the night before? Jenny must have suspected and might have told them. The girl was a clever one.

Jane made small talk, inquiring about their husbands and Graciela's small daughter, their health—both of them being with child—and the travel from Yorkshire.

"I've heard you're to attend the Kennerly musicale tonight," Sirena said. "I confess, when I looked over your wardrobe, I thought 'twould be better to have Madame give you one of the new gowns waiting here for you. Best to show up in the most current fashion, given that all the talk is of your disappearance. The scandal sheets mention it quite slyly, but you know how quickly the *ton* matches a name to a story."

She knew very well—she'd dodged that sort of attention for more than two decades. "Thank you," she said. "Madame, shall we go to your office?"

Guignard would arrive soon. She didn't wish to entertain him in front of this gaggle of ladies.

"I think we must," Madame said.

Barton rose. "I have your new gowns set aside, Lady Jane."

The door opened a crack and the shop assistant peeked in, her face tense. "A difficult visitor," the girl whispered.

La Fanelle frowned. "Barton shall be down just now."

The door floated all the way open. "No need," a male voice said.

Her heart fell. Kincaid's bulk filled the doorway.

Madame La Fanelle's face slipped into an unreadable coldness that matched his demeanor. And both were reaching into pockets.

She jumped in to join Barton between the two of them.

"Is there something we can help you with, Mr. Kincaid?" Barton asked calmly. Barton must have been introduced to the man at Shaldon House before she'd left Jane's employment.

Or…had Madame confided something about the man to Barton? The hostility between the Scotsman and the Frenchwoman was palpable.

Her nerves crackled at the tension.

He nodded, his gaze fixed on Madame. "You know why I'm here, Marie," he said.

"I'm the one you want to speak with, Kincaid," Jane said.

His gaze flitted to her and then back to Madame. "I'm

here, Marie, because that painting has put you and Barton and all your staff in danger."

What Shaldon knew, Kincaid would be told. Of course. She should have expected this.

Jane took a step closer. "It's not here."

His gaze narrowed on her. He looked almost quizzical. "Are you so sure?" he asked.

Was she?

"It is not," Madame said.

"The painting?" Graciela had risen. "*You* had it, Lady Jane?"

"What did those men on the road take?" Lady Sirena asked.

Her lungs squeezed with anger and panic. All of her efforts would come to naught. Shaldon would take the painting from her, and to get any money to help her son, she'd have to marry the man, and on top of that, she'd have lost the friendship and respect of his children.

She clenched her fists, and felt heat rising within her. She would have been found out anyway eventually. She would have lost their respect anyway. "The men on the road took a landscape," she said. "*I* transported Lady Shaldon's painting. I'm having it cleaned and reframed." She lifted her chin. "Lord Shaldon knows I mean to sell it."

A muffled cry on the stairs had Kincaid shoving the shop girl into the room and drawing a pistol. Madame pushed past Barton and Jane to join him, wielding a wicked pair of shears.

CHAPTER THIRTEEN

incaid disappeared into the corridor and came back supporting a slight figure.

Jane's heart dropped. *Guignard.* He'd lost his hat, and blood poured from his wizened old head, running down his leathery cheek onto a torn neckcloth.

Madame helped him onto a chair, handed Jane the shears, and began dabbing at the blood with a cloth. "Were you followed, Henri?"

"Devil take it, Marie, of course, he was followed." Kincaid turned on the shop girl. "Go and lock all the doors. Have one of the porters stand by and let only customers in. I'll be right along."

Madame nodded, and the girl hurried out.

"Lady Sirena, is your coach waiting outside?" he asked.

"It is."

"I'll ask you ladies to stay here for a bit and see to Guignard's injuries."

Kincaid vanished down the stairs.

"Some of that sherry," Jane said, signaling Sirena. She nudged Madame and returned the scissors. "Go see to the shop, Madame. Barton, you too. Send a girl up with water and bandages."

Sirena held the glass up to Guignard's lips. "Drink this, sir. Do you have other injuries, besides the gash on your head? There now, don't answer until you've taken another sip. Gracie, Madame keeps a bottle of Bakeley's best brandy somewhere. Have a look, will you?"

Jane bent close to Guignard, examining his wounds. He had taken a blow to the head, and there were other cuts and bruises around his cheeks and jaw. He favored an arm, clasping a hand to support his elbow.

"I'm so very sorry," Jane said.

The old man smiled, and she saw that one of his yellowing teeth had been broken. "It will take more than one of the Duque's bullies to vanquish Henri Guignard. And I was not followed."

"And what of the painting," Graciela asked. "Did they take it?"

He shook his head, a cough rattling up while his face turned red.

"Help me move him to the sofa," Jane said, "and have someone fetch a surgeon."

"I'm beginning to think the painting is cursed," Sirena said.

Her breath caught. "That it might bring bad luck to whoever transported it?"

"Yes."

"It's what I told Perry you would say. I fear you may be correct."

Sirena shook her head fiercely. "Never say it. I'm only a fanciful Irishwoman. We shall find a way to turn any bad luck to good."

. . .

"I CANNOT POSSIBLY GO TO THE MUSICALE TONIGHT," JANE said.

Madame removed a pin from her mouth. "You must."

Noise filtered up from the shop into the empty parlor. Kincaid and Marie had engaged in a heated discussion in rapid French—who knew Kincaid could speak the language so fluently?—in the modiste's private office, after which he'd sent for more guards, secured the premises, and escorted Lady Sirena and Graciela back to Shaldon House. Lady Sirena left on the promise that Jane would stay put at the shop until the Shaldon carriage came to convey her to the musicale, begging Jane to come home with them later to Shaldon House.

"Put out your arms. *Eh bien.* You will shine in this gown, my lady. *Gros de Naples* with embroidered net over it—it is very fashionable now, and the pale rose becomes you." She pulled on the skirts. "It is important to be out in society and to not show fear. Guignard will recover soon and cease to be mysterious."

Guignard, who was now reclining in Madame's bedchamber, following the surgeon's order to rest, swore that the painting was safe and promised that all would be well.

When asked to give its location, he had fallen into grievous moaning.

"Would he play us false?" she asked.

Madame's gaze met hers and the dark eyes were enigmatic.

Doubt slithered through her. Who could she really trust? And yet, the die had been rolled. She needed Madame's and Guignard's help. "It was probably Kincaid's presence that made Guignard reluctant to talk."

"No doubt." She helped Jane out of the new gown and

handed her a satiny robe. "But I assure you, if Guignard says the painting is safe, then it is. You will rest here on the sofa, and then Barton will help you dress later. Meanwhile, Jenny will go to Shaldon House for your evening slippers. Shall I have her carry along the gown you arrived in?"

"No. Have her take it back to Gerrard Street. I'm returning there after the musicale."

Madame pursed her lips. "I suppose Kincaid will have men watching that house now also."

"Very likely." Unless Shaldon himself came to make sure she was safe.

She shook off the excitement the thought stirred. She needed to think about her son.

Shaldon had offered him a position. Her best hope to keep Quentin out of Shaldon's clutches was to put herself into them. Not in a marriage, though. Now that he knew she'd taken his painting, a simple transaction—the painting for Quentin's debts, along with a promise to not embroil her son in his dangerous world—would suffice. Shaldon could flaunt his possession of the painting before the Duque and obtain his revenge, and she could render this final assistance to her son.

If she could persuade Shaldon to agree to it.

THE RED-HAIRED GROOM, EWAN, TROTTED UP THE STAIRS TO the shop to fetch her to the waiting carriage, and she had a moment of tingling apprehension.

Her slippers suddenly felt too heavy.

"My lady?"

Hazel eyes looked down on her. The boy had too many freckles and an air of dogged innocence. She took his arm and let him lead her. No fewer than four outriders followed the large town coach, and another groom rode on the back.

With one foot on the carriage step she froze. No lamp lit the dark interior and no gown shimmered in the light from the street.

A dark-clad arm and white-gloved hand reached out the coach door and snared her hand. "Shall we brave this, Lady Jane?"

Lord Shaldon tugged her onto the seat next to him.

It was her nerves making her prickly, he decided. The attack on Guignard had upset all the ladies.

"You did not expect me?" he asked. "No, I suppose not. At the last minute, Lady Perpetua sent a note that they would visit tonight, and the others decided to stay home. After the musicale, I'll escort you to Shaldon House so you may also visit with the newlyweds."

"I shall return to my lodgings tonight."

"You intend to stay there?"

"As long as Lady Hackwell will allow it." She sat primly, her hands locked together in her lap. "I suppose you've spoken to Lord Hackwell about the arrangement?"

"I sent a note regarding issues of safety. He assured me you may remain there as long as is needed."

She let out a breath and gazed out the window.

"Though I should like for you to return to Shaldon House." He reached for her hand. "I very much enjoyed our interlude last night. I will, I'm afraid, continue to importune you."

The tiniest of shivers went through her telling him that she'd enjoyed the night also.

But when she glanced at him, her expression was bland. "Thus scandalizing both the *ton* and your children."

He shrugged. "The *ton* flits from scandal to scandal. As for my children, they are all grown and happily married, and may keep to their own business." He slipped an arm around her back and slid his hands over the boning in her blasted stays. She was well turned out tonight in a pale, low-cut frock that showcased her fine bosom. "I've done my best for them in my own way, as you have for Penderbrook."

He could sense the tension rising in her and guessed at the emotion; exasperation, certainly, but also regret, perhaps even a grief he couldn't wholly understand. Though he'd been an absent father for most of his children's lives, it must be different for a mother.

And it wouldn't do for her to arrive in tears.

"I am trying to secure a position for him," he said.

Her head snapped around. "He told me. And he will *not* be one of your spies."

Memories rushed in. His bungling of a mission had ruined this woman's life.

Her revenge was to steal the painting from him. She blamed him for her brother's death. Hell, he blamed himself.

They were so alike, both of them holding their secrets close through the decades, waiting patiently for the chance to settle a score.

He didn't give a damn about the blasted painting. He'd give it to her, except that he needed it a bit longer to deal with the Duque.

"Did you hear what I said, Shaldon?"

What she said?

"My son will not be one of your spies."

He squeezed her waist. "No, he won't. I do not think he has the constitution for the work."

That caught her up and she swallowed whatever she was about to say.

"Your son, I believe, is too honorable for deception, much like his mother."

She shook her head. "You are forgetting my most recent theft, as well as the last twenty-five years."

"No, Jane. I always wondered why Cheswick never found you a husband. Now I know. You wouldn't present yourself to a man as an innocent, or hand over to a careless husband the funds that supported your child, or abandon the boy while you busied yourself with a new family. You practiced no deception. You merely kept a private matter private and honored your duty."

A shudder rolled through her and she leaned stiffly away from him.

He admired her obstinacy, though she hadn't yet realized his determination. Each act of resistance merely put them one step closer to her surrender. "As for the so-called theft, I understand all about that. I will help him, Jane, and you."

"Will you? Or, once you have the painting, will you send Quentin off on one of your missions and have me hanged?"

His wife would never hang, nor would her son ever make a spy.

*Once you have the painting...*Surely, she couldn't know all of his plans?

He'd underestimated her before.

His heart stirred, and he squashed a smile. "You will *not* be accused of theft. You don't have the painting, is that correct?"

"You know that I entrusted it to Guignard."

"With Madame's help." He cleared his throat. "There you have it."

She gasped. "You cannot mean to prosecute *them*?"

What a loyal creature she was. The idea had never crossed his mind. Still, he enjoyed poking her, and it was better for her to arrive with a high color from anger than weepy with worry.

He eyed her silently.

"If you try that, Shaldon, I shall turn myself in to the authorities and confess."

He squeezed her again. "Kincaid informed me that Guignard wouldn't tell you where the painting was located." Leaning closer, he whispered "What if it can't be found?"

Her lip trembled and he was instantly remorseful.

"Do not worry about your son," he said.

She sighed. "Well, I suppose if it can't be found, the treasure it maps will stay at the bottom of the sea, and then the Duque will come after *me*."

"The Duque shall not lay a hand on you or harm you in any way. And I suspect the treasure was ever a phantom, Jane. Captain Kingsley copied the coordinates and has been looking for it these many years." Their carriage stopped in front of a house glittering with light. "And now, my dear, we've arrived."

BLAST IT. SHE'D BEEN TOO ASTONISHED TO FIND WORDS TO negotiate a transaction with him. And he *would* tempt her with that tidbit of information about Captain Kingsley and leave out the rest of the story. Oh, he was a sly one, and surprisingly sanguine about the painting's location.

Too sanguine. He might trust Guignard to safeguard the painting as much as Madame did. Or he might himself know the painting's location. Or he might not care, because if the painting truly couldn't be found, then the Duque couldn't have it either.

For the Duque, the painting might represent treasure, but for Shaldon it meant revenge—as long as the Duque wanted it and couldn't have it. And if the painting was truly out of Shaldon's hands and lost, wouldn't that be a far better revenge against the Spaniard? Shaldon could go on with the rest of his life and be done with the Duque.

They climbed the steps to the salon where the musicians had assembled. Astonished gazes met their appearance together. Pretending to not notice the buzzing around them, Jane greeted acquaintances and allowed herself to be introduced to other guests.

They found seats and waited for the singer being featured, an Italian soprano newly arrived in London. Across the aisle from Shaldon, a large mustachioed man watched them through shifty eyes. He had an unsavory look about him.

She was grateful for Shaldon's presence.

"Who is that man?" Jane murmured.

Before he could answer, Quentin appeared, bowing over her hand and asking permission to take the empty seat on her other side.

He chatted politely about the singer and the evening's program. He was gentlemanly and polite and his good manners calmed her racing heart. If he hated her, he was hiding it well. Perhaps there was hope for her to be a real mother to him.

She saw the moment Quentin caught sight of the mustachioed man. He paled and his lips thinned, and he turned to greet the gentleman taking the seat next to him.

She touched Shaldon's arm. "Who is the man across from you?" she whispered again.

Shaldon craned his head toward the man and stared until the man broke the contact and turned away.

Her heart clattered within her. There was more afoot tonight then her conversation with Quentin.

"He's a sold-out major and I'm surprised he was invited. He's not someone I want to make my acquaintance." He touched her hand. "Or, if I may be so bold, my dear, yours."

When she glanced across the aisle again, the Major had disappeared.

At the interval, Shaldon sent a meaningful look to Quentin, and he in turn inquired whether she'd like some fresh air. Nerves rattling, she followed her son down a short corridor to an alcove overlooking the garden.

They were alone, the rest of the crowd having gone to chat with the soloist and to take refreshments.

Quentin began by thanking her prettily for agreeing to speak to him. It was rehearsed and stiff and she didn't know what to make of it until he sighed.

"I'm truly sorry for my reprehensible behavior yesterday," he said. "You have supported me all these years?"

"I've helped. I knew the Walkers would not be able to afford many luxuries. I chose them to raise you because they were said to be kind, especially Mrs. Walker. Nor were they fussy about official matters." She took a breath. More truth-telling. "Certain details of your baptismal record were forged, and they knew it." Mr. Walker's allegiance was to a higher authority than the state or even the episcopacy. "They were quite happy to pass you off as one of Mrs. Walker's distant relations. Were they kind, Quentin?"

"Yes. Kind and genteel, and firm, as I now admit was sometimes needed. My uncle—that is what I call him, is quite the scholar. My aunt was the salt of the earth. She died a few years ago."

"I heard and I'm so sorry."

He nodded. "It was unkind of me to speak to you so rudely. Lord Shaldon helped me to see that you've paid a price for...for me, whilst I lived quite comfortably. You may dispense with your support, though, because he has...he has seen to the debt and has offered me a position. So, you see, all will be well."

His smug smile, so like his disreputable father's, tore at the hole in her heart. She sucked in a breath and reached for his hand. "Quentin...your father...your father was Reginald Dempsey. He died never knowing about you. He was killed on one of Lord Shaldon's missions, along with my brother."

A breath of air, a slight noise, a sense of another presence, stilled her words. She'd lived most of her life attuned to such nuances and keeping her secrets.

In the distant music room, a violin wailed as a bow was dragged across it.

"I should like to know more, but we had better return to our seats," Quentin said. He clasped her hand between his. "And you're not to worry a bit about me. I'm perfectly capable of making my own way."

She walked numbly next to him, her hand tucked around his arm. He'd all but dismissed her until a more convenient time. Or perhaps Shaldon had already told him all of her story.

At the door to the music room she stopped. "I'm afraid I've a hem needing a stitch," she said, dropping her hand from his arm.

He bowed and went off, and when she turned, she almost bumped into a tall wall of muscle. The mustachioed Major blocked her way.

CHAPTER FOURTEEN

"*My* lady."

His smile was knowing and his eyes scanned her from head to toe, sending a cascade of cold dread down her spine.

She stood taller. "I do beg your pardon."

He cocked an eyebrow. "Do you?"

Up close, he was probably of an age with her. Perhaps he thought he was being engaging.

She stepped to the side and he matched her movement.

"This is not a country dance. Do move your insolent self out of my way so I may pass."

Eyes sparkling, he moved aside, and as she passed, he whispered, "When you tire of the puppy, I should be happy to linger in an alcove with you."

Hot wrath rose in her, but she moved one foot in front of the other and made herself walk calmly on.

FROM HIS SPOT BY A POTTED URN, SHALDON SAW JANE turn away from Penderbrook. Minutes later, Major Payne-

Elsdon entered, wearing a satisfied smile. Penderbrook had found his way back to their seats and was chatting affably with an acquaintance. For Penderbrook, the meeting had gone well, but Jane had pivoted away from the boy stiffly.

And then there was the appearance of the Major.

Shaldon caught Payne-Elsdon's eye and walked over. He'd prefer not having to get near this slithering bit of pond slime, but there was nothing for it.

"You're in good spirits, Major. Payne-Elsdon, isn't it?" Shaldon said.

The man bowed. "Lord Shaldon. Pleasure to make your acquaintance."

"Is it?"

"Met your son, Charles Everly, at White's."

"I see."

"I suppose he spoke of me and that's how you know who I am." His gaze narrowed. "Or, I suppose you make it your business to know many people."

"I thought we might have met," Shaldon flicked a spot of dust from his coat, "in Spain."

Payne-Elsdon blinked. It was just a beat, but one that a careful observer like himself would not miss.

"Oh? Were you there?" He laughed. "Nothing like it, is there? Warm weather, warm women, eh?"

Penderbrook had been in debt to this distasteful man? How careless of the boy.

"You're quite the swordsman, I hear."

The man smirked. "In both senses of the word. Haven't lost a duel yet." His gaze roamed the room and settled on a group of white-gowned girls. "Or disappointed a lady."

"No pistols at dawn for you, eh?" Shaldon asked.

He understood now the man's game with Penderbrook. Payne-Elsdon would insist on all the ancient protocols. He hadn't called Penderbrook out because under those rules the challenger didn't get to choose the weapon, and he wanted to fight with the sword.

Had Penderbrook spent time at Angelo's learning that skill?

Lady Jane appeared in the doorway, her face a set mask. Payne-Elsdon spotted her too and a feral light flashed in his eyes.

"You're a lucky man, my lord, escorting such a lovely lady tonight. Or is she under Penderbrook's protection?"

"The lady is esteemed by all the members of my large, extended family," Shaldon drawled, "as well as our friends, and the best society."

He turned his back on the man and walked away.

Payne-Elsdon was seeking to provoke a challenge. Someday, someone would have to kill him.

On the carriage ride home, Shaldon silently parsed Penderbrook's polite chatter about the evening's performance. With his debts paid, and his apologies made, the young man's cheerful self-assurance had returned.

In that regard, he was just like his father, Reginald Dempsey.

The present crisis was settled, but the boy's over-confidence, his cockiness, would provoke more to come. Had he not been stacked up against such a villain, and had it not been for Jane's involvement, he would have let the young fool flounder himself out of the pond and onto dry land.

The carriage pulled up in front of Penderbrook's lodgings.

"Thank you, my lord," he said. "I cannot thank you

enough for your generosity." He reached for Jane's hand. "And you, my lady, I should like to call on you soon and hear more of what you have to say."

It was all said too handsomely.

Without waiting for Jane's response, Penderbrook opened the carriage door and stepped out.

He turned and leaned in. "My lady." He fumbled his hat. "My lady, I was wondering if, in private, I may call you Mother?"

He felt Jane's sharp little breath and the jerk of her head as she nodded.

"Yes," she said. "I should like that very much."

Penderbrook's smile gleamed white in the light of a gas lamp. He closed the door and they pulled away.

JANE COLLAPSED AGAINST THE SQUAB, HER MIND A JUMBLE, her body conscious of Shaldon's warm bulk next to her and the possibility of his comfort.

His hand settled over hers. "Did it go well?" he asked.

Had it? How she wished to be close to the young man she'd thought about every day of his life. Still...he'd had twenty-four years of abandonment. He wouldn't have got over that so quickly.

"Perhaps too well," she said. "I think his anger yesterday afternoon was more honest."

"He is being courteous. Finding his way."

"He reminded me tonight of...of Reginald." She swallowed a lump and looked at him, making out his frown in the flashes of passing lights. "You paid his debt, he said."

"And he shall pay me a portion every quarter out of his salary."

"Such an amount, Shaldon—what sort of position will he

hold to allow that? He'll be tempted to more foolishness, or…"

"To theft?"

Shame welled in her, the heat of it rising into her cheeks. "I'll instruct Guignard to give you the painting if you'll forgive Quentin's debt and allow him to keep all of his income."

"The painting you stole from me?"

She held her breath, waiting for more and finally sighed. "Yes."

She would still be a thief, but she must at least try to give her son more of a future. And then she would find her own way.

And if her son was foolish again? A young man never had money enough.

If Guignard copied the painting before handing it over to Shaldon, she could sell that and add to her son's income.

"I am not opposed to the idea of selling the painting as you planned, but I believe it would be better to find an auction house that will take it on. A bidding frenzy might drive the price up." He squeezed her hand. "We will share the profits."

"You would allow that?"

"I've said so."

"Allow me to profit from my theft?"

"Your diversion kept the painting out of the hands of the thieves who assaulted my men on the road to Cransdall. Think of it as a commission."

A commission? She could perhaps pay off her son's debt, perhaps even arrange enough income that Quentin could someday marry.

But a public auction? "What if the Duque shows up to bid on it?"

"If the cost to the Duque is high enough, I might consider allowing him to attend."

"Surely, by now, he suspects as you do that there's no treasure to be found."

"He's a powerful opponent, but not the wisest of men. Do you remember Captain Llewellyn, the sea captain who threatened Graciela?"

"Yes." She had heard the story of Captain Llewellyn's villainy, though perhaps not all of it.

"He was allied with the Duque whilst pretending to be a friend to Graciela's father, Captain Kingsley. And Captain Kingsley spends part of his time hunting for sunken Spanish treasure and pirate caches."

"As well as privateering," she added. Graciela had brought a fabulous dowry into her marriage from Captain Kingsley's efforts. "You said he copied the coordinates."

He nodded. "Captain Kingsley presented me that painting years ago. Taken from a ship bearing treasures pillaged by the Duque de San Sebastian during one of his sojourns in New Spain."

Her breath caught. "He robbed the Duque of his treasures? Good heavens." So, the feud was a very long-standing one, with many players and tentacles.

"He relieved a great villain of his stolen booty. And I paid for that painting."

"And the treasure map."

His lips quirked. "I never believe such stories."

Well, and the Earl of Shaldon had treasures aplenty. No need to dive into the waters of the West Indies. "Has the Captain arrived back yet?"

"Not yet. I have a man in Portsmouth waiting to escort him here as soon as he comes into port."

Bringing Captain Kingsley swiftly to London would be a

great kindness to Graciela, but there were probably other reasons, reasons of state, to convey the captain to London so quickly.

These men and their endless plotting—her head ached thinking about it. And, no matter that Shaldon insisted otherwise, Quentin would become enmeshed in their games, her son who was reminding her so much of the father who had managed to get himself killed.

"You didn't tell me what sort of position you had in mind for Quentin."

"There are a few possibilities. What do you recommend, Jane?"

She'd had regular reports on her son, yet...what sort of man was he? "I don't think I know him well enough to say. But...out of London, certainly."

"Out of England?"

She sat up. If Quentin took a position out of the country, could she go with him, or at least live nearby?

The carriage turned a corner and she recognized the terrace of homes on Gerrard Street.

Shaldon said he'd enjoyed their tryst very, very much. Though he'd done no more than put an arm around her and hold her hand tonight, he would want to come up.

She wanted that also.

It seemed she'd lost control, not just of the painting, but of her good sense.

She straightened her spine. The first order of business was to not indulge herself with Shaldon again. She would be very firm with him tonight.

He escorted her to her door and a footman admitted them; a footman attired in the Hackwell livery, a footman who hadn't been there that morning.

Shaldon took her hand, turned it and bent over it,

pressing his lips to her palm. The warmth of his kiss permeated the delicate cloth of her gloves and sent a shiver through her.

"I leave you in good hands, my lady," he said. "Until later."

And then he left. The footman closed the door, and Jenny appeared from the shadows to walk up the stairs with her.

"His lordship scampered off quick enough," Jenny whispered. "Good that you'll get your rest tonight, my lady."

Jane stopped on the landing and pinned the girl with a fierce look.

Jenny curtsied. "Begging your pardon, my lady."

Her pardon, indeed. She stormed up the stairs, not sure who to be angrier with: Jenny, Shaldon, or herself.

CHAPTER FIFTEEN

*P*enderbrook watched the Shaldon carriage roll away, and then looked up at the door of his lodgings. It had been quite the day. Every morning for the last several days he'd awoken awaiting the challenge, wondering who might loan him a pair of pistols.

And then she'd shown up on his doorstep.

Shame and elation were all mixed together in his head. Shaldon's glove had been soft enough, but the Earl's dressing down had been direct. Honorable men did not risk more than their means. Honorable men did not insult ladies, especially one's mother who had sacrificed her own happiness for him.

The undercurrent was clear enough even for him—he could be a little thick at times when ladies were involved. Shaldon had saved him, and not because of Charley's request to help him. The old man was courting Lady Jane. His mother.

He wanted to laugh. He could be stepson to the great Earl of Shaldon, a by-blow to the lady, true, but look how

Shaldon had brought his own by-blow, Bink Gibson, into the fold.

Lady Jane had named his father as one Reginald Dempsey, a name he'd never heard before.

He glanced up and down the street. Lights still glowed in windows. It was early yet. Perhaps he could float the name Dempsey to someone discreetly at White's and find out if anyone knew the family. He'd heard that Charley had returned to town. Perhaps he would be there, having a drink and catching up with the fellows.

ATTIRED IN ANOTHER OF MADAME'S SHEER NIGHTGOWNS, Jane sat at the dressing table plaiting her hair.

She'd sent Jenny off to bed. She should take herself to bed, but...

Until later, he'd said. What did he mean? Would later be tonight? Or tomorrow?

He'd roused something in her, the irritating, insufferable, inscrutable man, and then he'd run off without satisfaction.

She paced to the fireplace, back to the bed, and then to the window. Distant carriage lamps bobbed down the street, moving from Covent Garden to Mayfair, others traveling in the opposite direction.

In the past several months while living at Shaldon House, she'd been more a participant in *ton* life than ever before. If she left England, she'd leave all of this behind. She truly didn't want to go.

If Shaldon *truly* would share the profits from the sale of the painting, she might have enough to live well without pinching pennies and economizing.

Could he really mean it, or was it just a way of bending her to his will?

Could he really care for her?

The next Lady Shaldon would take on at least two grand homes that required running, an army of servants to manage, social and charitable duties, four stepchildren and assorted in-laws and grandchildren, and a lord who promised to importune her in the bedroom.

An irritating, insufferable, and inscrutable lord. Also, nosy, managing, and manipulative.

No, no, she must count on securing her own future with a high auction price.

Many of the best in London were mad for art. The Duke of Wellington was a passionate collector. Perhaps if the work was properly restored, he would outbid the Duque. Wellington was as much a creature of competition and vanity as the rest of his peers. For him, obtaining the painting might be another victory over an ally of Bonaparte.

Tomorrow, she would meet with Guignard and discuss the matter. Or...

She walked back to the window and looked out. It had not been more than thirty minutes since she'd stepped out of Shaldon's carriage. London was still very much awake. At the modiste's shop, Madame would be up working on her accounts or a last-minute, urgent order. Guignard had planned to spend the night there.

The little Frenchman had rested the whole day. She wanted to know where he'd stashed her painting.

She tore through the clothes press, pulled out a chemise, tossed aside her stays, and found her traveling gown—the one gown she could get into on her own.

If Ewan tried to stop her, she would simply draft him to

come along as an escort. And then he could run off and tattle on her to his lordship.

* * *

PENDERBROOK SLIPPED PAST A TABLE OF WHIST PLAYERS, TOOK an empty chair near a stack of the day's papers, and ordered a drink. The crowd tonight was thin, some of the members trickling off to their country estates as the coronation festivities wound down.

It had been Charley, a true friend, who'd got him accepted as a member here, yet he'd found other friends from his days at school, some of them as lowly as himself.

"Join us?" a fellow called from the whist table.

"Not tonight," he said. "Has Everly been in?"

"Haven't seen him."

His drink arrived. He picked up a paper and scanned the reports of the King's proposed travel to Ireland.

Shaldon had mentioned a possible position abroad. He wouldn't want to find himself in Ireland though. Paris, Vienna, or Italy would be acceptable.

A shadow fell over his newssheet and he looked up.

"Fortune has favored you today." Major Payne-Elsdon's eyes gleamed in the lamp light. He took the opposite chair at the table. "Yet you're not joining the play."

He glanced over. One man was scribbling his vowels and departing. He doubted they'd want the Major replacing him. The man was widely believed to cheat, but no one had caught him out at it and no one wanted to duel with him. It was a certain thing that Major Payne-Elsdon would not delope with his shot. He would aim straight for his opponent's heart.

"No," Penderbrook said. He turned a page and skimmed the contents, unseeing.

The waiter appeared and Penderbrook shook his head at another drink.

"Come, Penderbrook. You've paid me off. Let me buy you a drink."

A chill rattled through him, a trickle of sweat sliding down the back of his neck. Like a damned rabbit he was when around Payne-Elsdon, always wandering into a trap. Everything with the man was a potential snare.

He glanced at the clock and set his paper aside. "I beg your pardon. Early day tomorrow."

Bowing he headed for the door, but Payne-Elsdon's voice rang out. "Off to join your new lady, are you?"

The room hushed, and he pivoted, bile rising in him.

"What a surprise to find you're Lady Jane Montfort's by-blow. By whom, I wonder?" Payne-Elsdon stood. "Now that she's Shaldon's bit, perhaps she'll give you a noble by-blow brother."

The hush around him was like a death watch. The events of that day and the one before flashed in his mind's eye, Shaldon's words echoing also. Honorable men did not insult ladies. Honorable men did not risk more than their means.

Lady Jane had given him life, and life was all he had to risk for her.

"Payne-Elsdon, you will cease defaming the lady."

"Or else?"

Heat rose in him. Certainty. It was, as Shaldon had said, time to step up and be a man.

"Look around," he said. "You, Payne-Elsdon, are not welcome at anyone's table. You measure your losses until the stakes are large, and then you *always* win. And one wonders how that can be. Though no one has caught you out...yet."

He waited. Payne-Elsdon smiled. "Your mother is a whore who left you on a parson's doorstep."

More sweat rose on his neck, belying the icy rage in his belly. "Lady Jane is no whore." He took a deep breath. "You and I will meet, Payne-Elsdon."

Under his oily mustache, the Major's lip curled. "Then I claim my rights as the man challenged. It shall be swords. Otherwise, I defer to all your wishes and await word from your second." He chuckled. "Best write your will. Shaldon won't rescue you this time."

"And you'd best loosen your neck cloth to make room for the noose. You might kill on the Continent with abandon, but your Spanish Duque won't rescue you from English justice."

He was aware of the aura of shock all around, the sudden quiet, and then the scrapes of chairs being pushed back, all the fools rushing to make notes in the betting book.

His world had come crashing down, but so be it.

"GOOD HEAVENS, EWAN." JANE PRESSED THE CORNER OF HER shawl to her nose, holding the hackney's stench at bay. The odor of strong cologne and stale tobacco she could stand, but the smell of recently cleaned vomit was almost too much.

"Best I could do." Ewan glowered at her in the dark.

Oh, she couldn't see his eyes, but his tone was unmistakable. He'd followed her out of the house and then she'd bullied him without mercy until he'd fetched this squalid conveyance.

"*Hmmph*," she said, hiding her relief that he'd done her bidding, not simply thrown her respectfully over his shoulder and forced her back to the house on Gerrard Street.

Shaldon would have no doubt sanctioned such a maneuver.

Traffic snarled around a brightly lit townhouse where a society event—a rout, a supper ball, a musicale—was being held. It was not a house she was familiar with but passing the throngs of gaily dressed ladies inspired black thoughts.

She was outside looking in again—the opposite was true of course, but with the stench of the coach swamping her, her mind was muddled with memories. Reginald had favored a strong cologne, and he'd smoked endless cigarillos.

And the vomit...heavens. She'd been sick from the moment her son was conceived and for entire months thereafter.

How funny that she could remember how Reginald smelled, but not his face. She squeezed her eyes shut and tried, but all that came to her was her father's popped eyes and his cold voice ringing out clearly.

My daughter, a trollop, chasing after a whoreson. And what did it get you but a bellyful and your brother dead because of you. You'll be a pariah, Jane, shut out. Respectable society won't have you near.

Heart pounding, she grabbed the seat as the hackney lurched through one crush and then screeched to a stop at another holdup.

Nausea rose in her, tightening her chest, constricting her breathing.

He'd been wrong, her father. Respectable society had accepted her. Whether they still would after her affair with

Shaldon became known, as it certainly must, was questionable.

As Lady Shaldon, her chances of acceptance would be better. She'd wear a countess's coronet and be wrapped in the earldom's respectability.

And she could almost feel the Earl of Shaldon's arms around her. Would it be such a bad choice?

The hackney rolled a few feet and then stopped again.

The thick fetid air was clouding her judgment. She reached for the door. "We'll walk the rest of the way." Stumbling out ahead of Ewan, she let him settle their fare while she caught her breath.

He offered his arm, still glowering, and they went down a mercifully quiet side street. Two unmarked black coaches had stopped in front of a darkened mews. No lights lit the interior, no grooms perched on the back. The coachmen sat poised to drive off.

The hair on her neck prickled, and she squeezed Ewan's arm and stopped him.

Quiet voices reached them. A gentleman walked out, darkly clad, his tall beaver hat hiding his hair, a woman on his arm. A lone street lamp caught sparkles from gems at the lady's throat, the silky swirl of her gown, and the gold of her hair. And the man's face.

Her heart thumped wildly, her breath catching. She pulled Ewan into a shadow and watched the Earl of Shaldon take the Duquesa de San Sebastian into his arms for a passionate embrace.

Her legs sagged under her and she settled onto a step.

"My lady." Ewan glanced over his shoulder, and turned back to her, his face grim.

"Shh." She took great gulps, trying to breathe.

He plopped down next to her, warm and sturdy and

mercifully speechless. They waited as coach doors closed and horses clomped away.

* * *

THE FAMILY PARTY HAD FINISHED BY THE TIME SHALDON returned home. His eldest, Bink Gibson, and youngest, Lady Perpetua, and their spouses had left, and the other ladies had also retired. His heir, Bakeley, and his youngest son, Charles, lounged in the library, a half-empty bottle of brandy at hand.

"No Lady Jane tonight?" Bakeley asked.

"She chose to stay at Hackwell's. She's savoring her independence." He pulled up a chair and ignored the smirk Bakeley sent Charles. "I'm glad you're both here. Tell me what you know about this Major Payne-Elsdon."

"If you recall, he was seen with the Duque's people in Southwark," Charles said.

"I do remember." Payne-Elsdon had been part of the group attempting to abduct Graciela, but he'd slipped away before the final confrontation.

"Of course you do, Father." Charles rolled his eyes and sat down near him. "He cheats at cards. Quite well, in fact. We've none of us been able to puzzle out how. But he wins a great deal and loses very little."

"He might just be good," Bakeley said.

"No. He's a villain. Excellent swordsman they say. It's well known that he's killed men in duels on the Continent." Charles drummed his fingers on the arms of the chair. "Gadding about France, Italy, and Spain, doing what, no one can say. He'd pick his marks, mostly wealthy young bucks, before dinner, and kill them before breakfast the next day for sheer sport, they say. He's been leaning on Penderbrook. I can't determine why."

He knew why. "I'm sorry to say, Charles, I believe it's because Penderbrook is your friend, and you're not fool enough to engage with him."

"So, it's a way of getting to you," Bakeley said.

"Or a way for the Duque to get to you." Charles swiped a hand through his hair. "Damn. We'll have to get Penderbrook away, and soon."

A tap on the door brought the butler, Lloyd. "A gentleman to see Mr. Everly," he said.

"At this hour?" Bakeley asked. "Who is it?"

"Mr. Penderbrook."

Blast it, but he'd dropped the boy at his lodgings. He'd refrained from ordering him straight to his bed only to spare the boy's dignity. Hell, he'd have been better to let him suffer embarrassment and spare his life.

Charles frowned. "We're too late."

"Indeed," Shaldon said. "Send him in, Lloyd."

Penderbrook entered moments later. In spite of the mild weather, perspiration rolled off his brow, his boyish face glowing red as he looked around, bowing to all.

"I beg your pardon." His voice cracked on the words. He cleared his throat. "I wonder if I might have a moment to speak with you, Charley?"

Shaldon pointed to a chair. "Sit down. You'll speak with all of us. Charles, get him a brandy. Bakeley, go and tell Lloyd to send for Kincaid."

While Bakeley went to the door, Penderbrook perched himself on the edge of the seat and accepted the glass from Charles. He stared at it a moment, took a deep breath, and tossed it back.

"Pour him another," Shaldon said, and watched as the amber liquid sloshed into the glass.

The boy gripped the tumbler with both hands and took a sip. "Thank you," he said, his voice restored to full manliness.

Shaldon settled back in his chair. "Now, Penderbrook, tell us what has happened."

PENDERBROOK RECOUNTED HIS RUN-IN WITH PAYNE-ELSDON at White's. The humiliation was as bad as Shaldon feared, inciting an angry gnawing in his stomach. Not only had Penderbrook been dishonored, but Jane's name had been besmirched—especially Jane's.

"I came to ask you, Charley, if you would appear on the field as my second."

A third glass of brandy had been required for that last bit of bravado.

"Yes, of course I'll second you," Charles said. "I've an excellent set of dueling pistols."

"You will not serve as second, Charles," Shaldon said. "I forbid it."

Penderbrook's face fell.

The door rattled open and they all turned.

"What's afoot?" Kincaid flipped a workman's cap onto the table and went to the sideboard, sorting through bottles until he found the whisky he favored. His worn trousers, dark jumper, and bedraggled neck cloth signaled that he had not been pulled out of his bed to appear here.

He turned and clomped over to an empty wing chair. "Never mind. I've heard the news," he said, raising his glass to Penderbrook. "Here's to your first outing, lad."

Penderbrook smiled wanly. Charles refilled his glass.

"What is the plan?" Kincaid asked.

Penderbrook squared his shoulders. "I'm going to die the day after tomorrow."

Shaldon's gaze met Kincaid's. His old comrade had been out investigating. He had news to report, but he wouldn't do it in front of the other men, and they first needed to deal with this puppy.

"Why wait until the day after tomorrow?" Kincaid asked. "Why not tomorrow?"

"You mean today?" Bakeley asked. "It *is* after midnight."

Penderbrook blanched. "That is mere hours away. I need time to find a second. To send letters and such." He downed the drink.

"There won't be any negotiating and apologizing," Kincaid said. "Payne-Elsdon won't come to peaceful terms. Best set the time to late morning—Battersea Fields is good. I'll have men clear a place for us. Mayhap the Major is out getting roaring drunk tonight, celebrating the success of the trap he's laid. Might put him off his guard to move things along quickly."

"I still need a second. Lord Bakeley—"

"No," Shaldon said. He glared at each of his sons and then settled his gaze on Penderbrook. "I'll serve as your second."

CHAPTER SIXTEEN

Shocked *Nos* came from the three younger men, but Kincaid nodded, eyes gleaming.

"My lord," Penderbrook said. "He's demanded swords instead of pistols."

"He would cling to that archaic rule," Shaldon replied. *The Major picked his marks before dinner and killed them before breakfast the next day.* "As Kincaid said, he'll not yield to negotiating anything that does not favor him, even the method of fighting. Penderbrook, Charles will see you up to one of the guest chambers. Bakeley, you will wake Penderbrook early and run through your latest practice from Angelo's."

"May I have paper and ink?" the young man asked.

Shaldon waved a hand. "Of course. Write out your will and whatever last missives that you wish, but don't be up until dawn doing it. You must get some sleep."

"I must also pay a call on Lady Jane. I fear I have left matters unresolved."

"No," Shaldon said. "Such a visit won't help you or her. You may speak to her after the duel."

"But—"

"Nor will you Bakeley, and you, Charles, discuss this matter with your wives. There is no need to upset the ladies. They will only want to rush out and interfere in what is a matter of honor between men."

When the door closed on the three younger men, Shaldon went to the sideboard. "A matter of honor with a murderer?" he muttered. "This has been a devil of a day."

Kincaid came over and refilled his own glass. "And another coming up. What's this particular devil up to, I wonder? The Major must know that if he kills that boy, you'll see him hang. Unless he thinks to delay his death by scampering off to Spain, but the Duque's business here isn't done yet."

"This is blood sport to Payne-Elsdon." Shaldon tipped back a swig that banished the chills.

"Blood sport for him, and for the Duque, a poke at you."

"The Duque doesn't care if Payne-Elsdon dies or he hangs." He thought about the intelligence he'd received after delivering Lady Jane to her lodgings. "And he won't—hang, that is."

Kincaid's gaze wandered to the cold fireplace and he squashed a smile. Dispensing cold justice was one of his favorite endeavors. "Let's just make sure the boy doesn't hang either," Kincaid said. "Or you."

"We won't. I've met with the Duquesa tonight, and I believe she might facilitate a trip to Spain for the Major."

Kincaid raised an eyebrow, waiting.

"The Major left many enemies."

"And revenge would make for some perfect justice. What's next?"

He took a sip of the stiff whisky. The brew made by Kincaid's people in the north wasn't considered a gentleman's drink, and he didn't give a damn. "Did you take care of those matters with Guignard?"

"Aye."

"Is he safe?"

"Still bunking at Marie's. She'll have his head later."

"She'll have your head."

Kincaid turned away and went for the whisky bottle, but not soon enough. Only the oldest of friends—like himself—could have detected the whiff of pleasure given off by the man.

Bloody hell, they were a couple of old fools.

But not too old or too foolish to get a young fool out of a pickle. "Do we have a servant in place at Payne-Elsdon's lodgings?" Shaldon asked.

"Aye. More than one, in fact. Has the bastard picked his second?"

"One will step up after Payne-Elsdon receives my letter. Will you carry it?"

"Write it out while I go arrange for the surgeon."

"I'll have one more note to carry to the Duquesa. Have someone stand by to run messages tonight. I fear we won't get much sleep."

"We've gone sleepless before." Kincaid plopped his empty glass on the sideboard and walked to the door.

"Kincaid?"

His old friend paused.

"Stop by and roust our apothecary out of his warm bed. I've in mind a tonic we used once in Bavaria. Do you remember the one?"

Kincaid grinned and left.

. . .

A SHORT WHILE LATER, SHALDON FINISHED CONSULTING WITH Lloyd, sent Kincaid off with his first round of formal letters, and made his way to his bedchamber.

Should he change and visit Gerrard Street?

Her words came back to him…she was not too old for their coupling to have consequences. One more document must be prepared.

When he entered his bedchamber, he found Charles there, sprawled in the chair by the dead fireplace, eyes closed. His youngest son would make one last attempt to wrest this obligation from him.

When the door clicked closed, Charles shot to his feet.

"Have you seen to Penderbrook?" Shaldon asked.

"I gave up and left him in the care of a patient footman. He's still scribbling letters. Morose as hell and determined to die like a man. He's begged me to help him sneak away in the morning to see Lady Jane. Won't believe I don't know where she is."

"Your wife hasn't told you? She's at Hackwell's vacant townhouse on Gerrard Street."

He blinked, no doubt absorbing the notion that Graciela had held back the secret. A grin split his face. "Good God. By herself?"

"Jenny is with her. And we've added other staff for her safety."

"Perhaps…perhaps, Father, you should go stay with her tonight."

Only years of practice allowed him to hide his astonishment. And pleasure.

Charles squeezed his hands into fists. "There's certainly the chance of danger for her, with Payne-Elsdon bringing up her name. Perhaps the Duque has discovered her connection to the painting." He cleared his throat. "Sirena said you were...you were out all night last night, and that you've, er, asked Lady Jane to marry you."

He loosened his neck cloth and tossed it aside, suddenly fatigued. Not ready for his bed though. He'd rather catch his second wind in the night air.

A dark jumper and coat had been set out for him. Should he don them, or not?

Charles walked closer and braced a hand on the mantel. "Which we all agree will be capital. Gracie did find it odd that Lady Jane wept so much at our wedding." He shook his head. "But of course—she'd just met her son. I suppose you're right though. It would be odd for Penderbrook to call on her in the early morning. She'll know, the way the ladies always seem to know, that something is wrong, and she'll winkle it out of him. Then she'll demand he not fight, they'll argue, and he'll go away doubting himself. Best to let her know in a letter he cared for her."

"He's not going to die tomorrow."

Charles huffed. "Father. You *don't* mean to fight in his place?"

He turned away. He would fight and he would win.

"But...a man of your age? And Penderbrook *must* appear. His honor...he'll be called a coward...you don't...Father? What are you planning?"

What he was planning needed more thought. He needed Charles to leave.

He needed Jane. He needed her in his arms, in his bed.

And what if she *winkled out* the news of the duel from him? She'd already blasted through years of stoic reserve. She'd turned him into a young fool all over again.

He sat down in the chair and began removing his shoes.

Charles went down on one knee next to him. "Let me take on this battle tomorrow, Father."

"A man of my age, Charles? *Really*? And as I recall, Bakeley is far better with a sword than you." The second shoe came off. "Do not worry. Unless I'm knocked down on my way there by some fool in a speeding phaeton, I don't plan on dying tomorrow, either."

Charles gazed at him, his face uncharacteristically solemn. The boy had his mother's coloring, her lighter brown hair and amber eyes. Charles was, in many ways, the child he was closest to, given the boy's stint on the Continent digging up secrets for the Crown.

"If Penderbrook won't die, nor will you, does that mean Payne-Elsdon will?" Charles got to his feet. "Unless...do you need him alive?"

"I doubt he has anything of value to offer us. But, he will leave the field alive. As it turns out, the Duquesa has a use for him."

Charles's mouth dropped open, and then he laughed. "Or her father does. I am glad I ended with her on friendly terms."

"As am I." Charles had pretended to be the Duquesa's lover, passing messages through her to her father, a powerful Spanish count, and no friend to the lady's husband.

"Have you fought duels before, Father?" He swiped a hand through his hair. "Oh, what am I asking? Of course, you have."

"I've fought too many times to count, but not gentlemanly affairs." He'd sparred with sharp stilettos in Italy, brawled with fists and feet in the alleys of Paris, and discharged pistols at Bonaparte's agents at close range and far. And those were the physical confrontations.

"It's no gentleman we're dealing with tomorrow, Father. How can I help?"

GUIGNARD SAT ACROSS FROM HER, CLOTHES NEATLY PRESSED, neck cloth starched, hair pomaded. The rest of him—hollow cheeks, sad eyes, gnarly hands—was rumpled with age and rascally living.

"My lady," he said. "It is not that I am trying to keep secrets."

It had been thus since his arrival in Madame's parlor, after she'd waited impatiently for hours during his *toilette*.

She eased in a breath and reached deeply into her nest egg of patience—which after so many years of withdrawals, was almost bankrupt.

Quiet footsteps on the stairs signaled Madame's approach. Perhaps Madame could lean on her cousin to tell Jane where the painting was hidden.

She wasn't leaving this room until she knew where to find it. She needed to know the painting was safe, that she could sell it or copy it, or otherwise profit from it.

She needed to know she wasn't being tricked or betrayed by this man also.

"Keeping secrets is exactly what you are doing, Monsieur Guignard," she said.

"I assure you, it is safe."

"I thank you. Now, please tell me *where* you are safeguarding it."

"The knowledge might endanger you, my lady."

"*Good heavens.* I carried the painting all the way from Yorkshire. Just tell me."

The door creaked open with a wisp of a draft, but she kept her gaze pinned on the little Frenchman.

"Tell her, Guignard."

Heart thumping wildly, Jane fought for a breath.

Shaldon was here.

CHAPTER SEVENTEEN

*H*is lordship had left the arms of his beautiful lover and come here.

The nerve. The absolute nerve. He'd left one woman to track down another.

And did he think she'd welcome him into her bed?

He came to stand next to her, dressed all in black like a housebreaker, the coat hugging his muscled frame.

After meeting his lover—his *other* lover—he'd gone home and changed his clothing. Had he dressed like that to break in to see her again?

"My lord." Guignard stood, licking his pale lips.

"It's all right, Guignard. Tell Lady Jane."

Guignard turned sad eyes upon her. "My lady. The masterpiece is now with Lord Shaldon."

Jane shot to her feet and then plopped down again, a haze forming before her eyes.

"Of course." Her voice shook on the words.

She should have known.

She'd been betrayed again. Lied to. He would split the

profits from the sale, would he? He'd spoken with such assurance because he'd taken control of the painting.

She was a *fool*.

"Always one step ahead, are you not, Shaldon?" Numbness crept up her arms. She pumped her fists, trying to get sensation back into them. "Always one step ahead of *me*."

Always one step ahead of everyone.

She mustered a breath. "So, you took his lordship's gold sovereigns, Guignard?" Her voice shook again, and *damn it*, she didn't care. Bile rose in her and she swallowed it back, forcing her fists to uncurl. She wanted to stand, she wanted to leave. Let Shaldon play his bloody games without her. Let him do as he pleased with her foolish, unappreciative son.

"Not yet, my lady." Guignard's voice came faint and from far away.

Black dots sprinkled Guignard's face. She squeezed her eyes shut and gulped in air.

"Jane." Shaldon spoke into her ear.

His hand pressed her back. "Take another deep breath," he said.

"*Damn you*," she choked out. His hot strength enveloped her, tempted her, angered her. She squeezed her eyes tighter, resisting.

When she opened them, Guignard and his black dots were gone.

Shaldon was still there, gripping her hand and watching her, that vein pulsing again in his temple. He was down on one knee. Not, she noted, the mangled one.

Heat rose in her. She'd been naked with him, she'd made love to him, slept with him. She'd given herself to him, fully. And all the while he'd been dallying with someone else.

It was happening again, *damn it*.

Heart pounding wildly, she yanked her hand away and gulped in more air, reaching for sanity.

It had been only one night, after so many years of being so good. Tears brimmed, and she squeezed her eyes shut.

Only one night, one night that meant *nothing* to him. It must mean nothing to her.

And it didn't. She wasn't a raw young girl any more. She'd not given her heart, no matter that he'd asked for it.

Had she, in those intimate moments, revealed something, some piece of intelligence that had led him to Guignard?

"You visited my bedchamber last night to find the painting."

"No." He swiped a hand through his hair. "In any case, Kincaid made the connection between Guignard and La Fanelle."

"Did you secure the painting before you dallied with me then?"

"I was not dallying. I am deadly serious about marrying—"

"You are dodging my question."

He straightened.

"Oh, do get up, Shaldon, and for once, *tell me the damned truth.*"

He blinked. "It was after."

Bile rising again, she pressed a hand to her mouth. Before or after, what did it matter?

She stood, drawing him up by the elbow. "Get up. And pray, tell me, what lady would want to marry a man like you, always planning, and plotting, and scheming? You would be up and off for...for South America, or...or India, tracking down someone who did you wrong decades ago, flying off with not so much as a note of goodbye."

He opened his mouth and closed it, his expression inscrutable.

No denials then? Heat pounded into her head, anger sparking along every muscle.

"Or maybe your lady won't care, because if you're off swanning around other parts of the world she won't be confronted with the three or four different women you're tupping as you carry out your revenge."

"Jane."

"What lady wants a husband, much less a lover, who would escort her home from a musicale and be off to make love to another, *all in the same night?*" She shook her fist at him and squeezed her eyes shut blocking out his astonished look. "*Not I*, Shaldon. Not I. I'll not marry you. I'll not play second fiddle to your cronies and chums, and all the sneaking old enemies from twenty years in your past, or to the women you're bedding for England. Take the blasted painting. Go and wave it under your Duque's nose while you cuckold him."

He took in a sharp breath. "*Jane.*"

Soft linen touched her cheek.

Blast it all. She was weeping.

"Look at me, Jane." He pressed the handkerchief into her hand and secured her shaking shoulders, his hands infuriatingly gentle, his dark gaze locked on hers. "The painting is *all* yours. Do with it as you please. There is no other woman, most definitely not the Duquesa. I did not make love to her." He pressed his lips together, looking almost nervous. "Marry me, Jane."

"No."

"Take some time. Think about—"

"No. There's no need for time." *No need, no need, no need.* She must be off, and soon. "The answer is no."

Pain flashed in his eyes, quickly shuttered.

Had she seen that? Had that been real? Or was it another one of his deceptions and tricks?

Oh, how she wished it wasn't.

She shook her head. "I'm leaving, Shaldon." Perry would loan her the funds, or Sirena, or perhaps Graciela. "This is only a game for you...a challenge. You don't truly want *me*."

His steady gaze sent warmth rippling through her, stirring up echoes of the previous night's pleasure.

"I want you," he whispered. "You've lived in my home for months, tempting me. This is no game. I care for you. I would be true to my vows, to you, always. I can be as loyal as you, Jane. Please. Give my proposal twenty-four hours. We'll talk tomorrow night. Will you agree to that much?"

True to his vows, and lying to her right now? She'd seen him with the Duquesa, with her own eyes.

And yet...and yet...

"Please, Jane. Please do not leave me yet."

Hot tears rushed her eyes. That had been heartfelt. And what a pathetic watering pot she was becoming.

She nodded. "I couldn't possibly put together an escape that quickly."

He leaned in and his lips touched hers, warm and firm.

And then he was gone.

Jane staggered to the sideboard where Madame kept her sherry and poured a drink.

Monsieur Guignard entered on a cool draft of air that made the tapers flicker. He was carrying the gold-painted rolling pin, the one she had used as a case for the painting.

"My lady, my betrayal was unavoidable I'm afraid. But I believe, nevertheless, that we shall both receive better benefit from the new arrangement, and a certain level of *sécurité* far better than had we acted on our own. And should you still feel the need for funds to leave the country, I have something here that I hope will restore your trust in Monsieur Guignard."

He pried the lid from the tube and slid out a rolled canvas.

Her breath caught as she unfurled it, her pulse accelerating.

The varnish was not as cracked as the original—but a buyer might think it was the original that had been restored. The row of numbers still ran along the crimped yellowed edge.

"It's brilliant." She glanced up at Guignard. "Or...is this the original? Did you give Shaldon a copy?"

He shook his head. "I would not presume to deceive that particular earl. I know of a dealer in Flanders who will be happy to look at this. We can sell it to him for a good price."

"We?" Guignard obviously thought he was coming with her to the Continent. She supposed she would need someone's help if she meant to sell off a copy as the original.

Unless she sold it here before leaving. She could give Guignard his commission, and give a portion to Quentin, though he wouldn't need it if Shaldon had paid his debt and found him employment.

She smoothed the canvas again. Quentin had made his indifference clear—he didn't need her help. What could she have expected after years of estrangement and neglect?

Staying in England, with Quentin ignoring her and Shaldon importuning her while he carried out his other affairs would be intolerable. But traveling to the Continent with Guignard? No...just...no.

"You may help me sell it here," Jane said.

"But to whom?"

She straightened her spine and walked to the window.

The sun was up, the shopkeepers were opening, and carts of goods rumbled in the street below.

It was only a copy. She would start with the obvious client.

"HE IS NOT IN."

The stuffy porter at Mivart's Hotel had taken her name and examined her closely before allowing her and her two companions, Guignard and Ewan, across the establishment's threshold.

She'd refused a new gown, but Barton had found her suitable undergarments for this mission and covered her tightly coiled plait in a fashionable bonnet. She was presentable for Mivart's and its noble clientele.

"My lady." Guignard tugged at her sleeve. "We should not bother the D—"

"When would be a good time to call?" Jane asked the porter. It was early of course for the aristocracy, but mid-morning was not too early for a matter so urgent. She couldn't put together an escape in one day, perhaps, but she could make a good start on her plans once she had money.

Guignard had discouraged her attempting this negotiation, insisting he would take care of everything. As if she would ever again fully trust him.

"If you would leave a note I shall see that he receives it."

"Very well," she said. "But the matter is urgent. You must see that he receives it immediately upon his arrival."

A lady appeared on the staircase, her blonde hair peeking out from under a bonnet in a shade of blue that perfectly matched her dress.

Jane recognized the design from a similar one in

Barton's sketchbook. She recognized the lady as well. It was early for such a lady to be up and about.

She dipped into a curtsy worthy of Spanish nobility. "Duquesa," she said. They had been introduced at the same diplomatic ball where her husband had insulted Graciela.

The Duquesa de San Sebastian inclined her head and extended her hand. "Lady Jane Montfort. It is a great pleasure." Her gaze swept up the porter, Guignard, and Ewan. "Leave us."

The porter hustled Guignard and Ewan outside. The dark-clad maid and the two men who had appeared behind the Duquesa stepped back out of earshot.

Jane fought for composure. The lady was exquisitely beautiful. It was no wonder Shaldon had hastened from her bed to the Duquesa's, like a horseman changing from a cob to an Arabian stallion.

But she must go on. "I was hoping to speak with the Duque about a matter of business."

For a lady to visit a nobleman on business was impertinent, brazen, and not done, but she didn't care.

Could she share the nature of the business with Shaldon's paramour? No doubt the Duquesa's relationship with Shaldon was as mercenary as her own.

She had come to sell the Duque the copy Guignard had provided, but perhaps she should offer it to the Duquesa.

The lady's blue gaze rested on her and it was not unkind.

She squared her shoulders. She wouldn't swindle the Duquesa. She wouldn't negotiate the sale of the forgery Guignard carried in the small satchel he was clutching. She would hold Shaldon to his word and act as his agent to sell the authentic painting *he* held.

The Duquesa raised an eyebrow. "You are here regarding this painting the Duque covets?"

Jane let out a breath. "Yes."

"Lord Shaldon's? Yes, of course." The lady paused, opened her mouth, closed it, and opened it again.

Choosing her words carefully, Jane thought.

"I have no interest in the painting. My husband, he is off this morning to attend an affair of honor."

"An affair of..."

Her chest tightened. An affair of honor—a duel.

Under the lady's gaze, her scalp began to warm and prickle.

"Whose?" Jane blurted the question.

The Duquesa inclined her head and reached for Jane's hand, squeezing it and letting go. "That is all I may say." She whisked out the door, her maid and guards following her.

After she'd left, Guignard, Ewan, and the porter pushed in.

Heart throbbing, Jane let herself be led out to the street. She turned on Ewan. "What do you know of a duel this morning?"

The boy blinked, and he shook his head. "Naught, my lady."

"Guignard?" she asked.

"I also know nothing."

Penderbrook's debt had left him in danger of a challenge, but Shaldon had paid his debt, he'd said. Had the foolish young man concealed other debts? Or incurred more?

She signaled the hackney they'd left waiting and gave an address near Berkeley Square.

"Where are we going?" Guignard asked.

"Shaldon House." Ewan said, and she heard the relief in his voice.

CHAPTER EIGHTEEN

"I hope this plan works." Bakeley looked up from the legal document he was perusing. Perspiration still burnished his brow from his practice session with Penderbrook, but his neckcloth was perfectly knotted, and he looked as though he'd had a few moments of sleep, unlike the rest of them.

"Father is a dab hand with plans," Charley said. "It will work."

Or it had better. Charley set a fresh bottle of brandy next to Penderbrook's *Last Will and Testament*, the document hastily prepared earlier by one of Shaldon's solicitors.

"He's leaving half of everything to Lady Jane, and the other half to a Mr. Walker."

"The clergyman who raised him. Where's Father?"

"Off with Kincaid sharpening the swords," Bakeley said. "He trundled in late last night."

"In the wee hours?" Had he been sharpening his other sword at Lady Jane's?

He laughed and pressed a hand over his face, trying to blot out that awful image.

Bakeley laughed also and shook his head. "I find I don't mind the idea of Lady Jane."

"If she bolts now and then, he'll stay out of our hair."

"Exactly." Bakeley's gaze sobered. "If our people at Payne-Elsdon's lodging fail us, is he better than the Major?"

"I don't know. I imagine Father knows a trick or two, and is willing to use them, damn the rules. And if all else fails, you'll step in as *his* second to enforce honor with your trusty pistol, and Kincaid will have his throwing knives. And we could call in Bink with his deadly left hook. I, of course, will be in the bushes with Pender, spewing my morning breakfast, all in the name of preserving our cover." Charley cracked his knuckles. "I suppose I'll understand better what Gracie's going through."

Bakeley's gaze held his for a very long pause. "You broke Father's rule and told your wife."

Charley grinned. How astute Bakeley was becoming. Almost a mind-reader. His wife was able to keep secrets. On the other hand...

"You told Sirena."

Bakeley's mouth firmed, and Charley laughed. "We are both disobedient churls. I hope you locked your lady in her room, else she'll be dashing out the door looking for Lady Jane. And why am I laughing? Gracie will be right by her side, more than likely."

"Sirena is sworn to secrecy," Bakeley's eyes flashed a warning.

He held up his hands. "Don't call me out, brother. I know your lady can keep secrets too." His sister-in-law had almost been killed in this library because of a secret. "With another lady's heart at stake, we've led our wives into terrible temptation. How long will they hold out?"

"Long enough I hope," Bakeley said.

The library door opened, and Penderbrook stepped in, scanning the room as if it was the last time he'd ever see it.

"Come and sign, Penderbrook," Bakeley called. Ever the man to get down to business, was his brother.

Bakeley explained the hastily prepared document while Charley found a corkscrew and opened the bottle of brandy.

"You're as white as your neck cloth, Pender," he said. "That won't do."

Penderbrook ignored him as he scrawled his name, and Charley went to fetch three glasses.

"None for me," Bakeley said. He blotted the document and set it aside. "Your letters?"

Penderbrook pulled a stack of missives from an inner pocket and Bakeley stacked them atop the will.

"What the devil, Pender?" Charley said. "Did you write to every man at the club? Or are those just your former creditors?"

Color rose in his friend's cheeks, just as he'd hoped it would.

"We need to leave in minutes. I'm going to find Father," Bakeley said, and walked out.

Charley poked his friend's shoulder. "I'm a scoundrel, I know, but I'm a true friend. A little angry spirit will serve you well, just don't unleash it on me. Now." He filled two glasses with generous pours. "Bakeley has shared a bottle of his spirits from his best hidden cache. As that happens very seldom, you must partake, and I, as your friend, will join you."

Penderbrook reached for the glass, then hesitated. "Perhaps I'd better not."

"You're shaking Pender. Take the glass."

Penderbrook looked at his hand, sighed, and obeyed.

Charley clinked glasses. "To your first outing." They tossed back their drinks.

"Hmm," Charley mused, refilling their glasses. "I do believe I'll need to filch the butler's key and help myself to more of this."

Penderbrook took the new glass and studied the amber liquid. "It has a different flavor."

"Aged," Charley said, sipping. "Smooth, though." Smooth with just a hint of the herbs that were added.

"Yes." Penderbrook drank down the whole glass. "Thank you, Charley."

Footsteps clacked in the hallway. "One more," Charley said, pouring.

The door opened, and Kincaid poked his head in. "Almost ready?"

Charley held up a finger and they both drained their glasses. He clapped Penderbrook on the back and smiled. "Now we're ready."

As they pulled up to Shaldon House, Jane bolted from the carriage behind Ewan and handed her coins to the boy. "Have the driver wait."

Guignard was climbing down, and she tugged the bag from him, passing it to Ewan. "You'll hold this. Don't let it out of your sight."

At the front door of Shaldon House, the porter bowed and greeted her.

"Lady Sirena," she said. "Where is she?"

He blinked—the only evidence of surprise—and stepped back. "In the morning room, my lady," he said.

Jane ran up the stairs to the back parlor and burst in, panting.

"My lady." Jenny rushed over. "Thank God. You left without waking me. I was looking for you."

Sirena and Graciela came and each took one of her hands. "They left not five minutes ago carrying their swords," Sirena said. "We didn't know what to do."

"We were sworn to secrecy," Graciela said. "And we didn't truly know what it was about."

"But I heard all about it from one of the shop boys, who heard it from one of the kitchen boys at White's," Jenny said. "I didn't know where to find you."

"The duel," Jane squeezed both ladies' hands. "Who is fighting?"

"That villainous major," Sirena said. "And Penderbrook."

Her heart pounded fiercely, the noise of it filling her head. After all her care, all of her sacrifices, it had come to this.

"Jenny," Sirena said, "pour Lady Jane some tea."

"No tea. Where did they go? What time?" He could already be dead, her son.

She'd barely had a chance to know him.

She was led to a sofa and a warm cup was pressed into her hands.

A vision of the Major's face the night of the musicale reared. "He's a brute," she said. "He'll kill him." The cup rattled, tea sloshing as she set it down. "Shaldon paid the debt. How can this be?"

Sirena shared a look with Graciela and bit her lip.

"Mr. Penderbrook challenged *him*, my lady," Jenny said.

"*What?*" The fool. The damned, stupid fool. "*Why?*"

The ladies exchanged another glance and Sirena sighed. "He insulted you."

Jane shook her head. "So? Is that worth dying for?"

"My lady, he insulted you publicly at White's," Jenny said.

"All the gents heard. It's all anyone speaks of. The Major called you a...beggin' your pardon, my lady...a whore."

She squeezed her eyes tight. Every so-called gentleman in London, every servant, every shopkeeper, *everyone*, was passing around that story.

She took a deep breath. "And perhaps it's true. Quentin Penderbrook is my son. Born out of wedlock. I...confessed it to him the day before yesterday."

Sirena's eyes flashed fire. "You could not have been much more than a child."

"Like I was." Graciela squeezed her hand. Her own little girl had been born illegitimate. "By their rules it is true, Lady Jane, but not by ours, as you know."

"There's more," Jenny said. "He called you Lord Shaldon's...er...*bit* was the word used, they said."

She took a deep breath and looked up at the carved molding that ran along the coffered ceiling. A soft hand clasped hers.

"It would explain why he's been more...congenial. We hope it is true," Sirena said. "We would be happy to see you become the next Lady Shaldon."

"Yes," Graciela said. "That would make you our mother." She laughed and then sobered. "But it is not a laughing matter, this duel. At least they are fighting with swords. It's a bit fairer if a man has some skills."

A chill seeped into her spine. "I have no idea whether Quentin has any such skills. Does Charley? He is his second, is he not?"

"No."

"Bakeley, then?"

"No," Sirena said. "Shaldon forbade it. 'Tis an honor he's taken as his own."

"*Shaldon?*" Jane jumped up and paced to the window.

Shaldon was...old. Oh, he was still vigorous, and a big man, and still strong, but the Major was larger, younger. If her son didn't fight, Shaldon would.

She couldn't bear losing either one of them. She must stop them.

Loud voices in the corridor drew their attention. Lloyd eased the door open, his face a stoic mask, and stepped out of the way for a dark-haired man of middle-age, dressed in a coat shiny with wear and dusty knee breeches.

Graciela choked out a breath and flew at the new arrival shouting *"Papa."*

CHAPTER NINETEEN

Shaldon peered out the coach window, but all he could see were the riders escorting them.

"Are we late, sir?" Penderbrook asked. His voice had been strong when they left Mayfair. Now the words came as though strained through a sieve.

Charley's mount moved out of the way and he spotted a group across the field: three men—no a fourth and fifth hovered along the sidelines.

Penderbrook's eyes widened and he put his hand to his mouth.

"We are in good time," Shaldon said. "You will stay near the coach with Charles and Bakeley. I am going to talk to his second. He will want to use a saber or broadsword, but I'm going to argue for our lighter weapons." The heavier sword would benefit the heavier man, Payne-Elsdon. He had hopes, after Bakeley's report, that, should Penderbrook's stomach prove iron-clad, the young man could carry on at least for a bit with the small sword. It appeared that the scholarly vicar hadn't neglected that part of a young gentleman's training.

When the coach stopped, he pushed open the door and let Penderbrook stumble out first.

Kincaid reached into the coach from the other side and picked up the two sheathed blades. "*He* is here."

Angry energy simmered in him. He drew in a breath, thinking of Jane, of her loveliness their night together, of her passion, and her grief. She needed a champion today. The energy must be kept, the anger let go.

He straightened his coat and looked at the terrain. Payne-Elsdon had claimed a high ground for his headquarters. The field in between their carriage and his position was grassy and probably dotted with hidden holes.

A Captain Shaw had replied to the rigorously polite letter Shaldon had written the Major making the arrangements, following the proper etiquette for this nonsense. Through the night and wee hours, a back and forth of missives had ensued, with Shaw agreeing to make a final judgment on the precise choice of weapon before the match began.

As he approached the group across the field, a thin mustachioed man broke away from the Major and walked toward him. He was pale and patting his mouth also.

Excellent.

Shaldon bowed and ignored the hand offered for shaking. He turned and beckoned Kincaid.

"I am Shaldon," he said. "Are you Shaw?"

"Yes."

"We have brought the *epees.*"

Kincaid stepped forward and unsheathed both weapons.

Shaw glanced at them. "As I informed you, the Major claims the choice of weapon. He wishes to fight with a broadsword."

"He is the man who delivered the gravely unnecessary

insult." Shaldon leveled a hard gaze at him. "An uncivilized, ungentlemanly, and uncouth insult. The Major is the stronger man, is he not? And yet he plots to overmatch his opponent with a heavy weapon? Is he afraid of his challenger's skills, or is he just a murderous bully?"

A green pall came over the man. He took the proffered weapon and bowed. "I shall talk to the Major."

"Had a bit of the bottle himself, do you think?" Kincaid murmured.

Not far from the Major and Shaw, a dark-suited man, probably their surgeon, was biding his time. The fourth man on the field today, paunchy and over-dressed, stood off to one side, a liveried guard nearby.

"Are you keeping an eye on that *epee*, Kincaid?" Charles had stepped up next to them.

"Aye. If he does anything more than slide his fingers down it and whisk it in the air, I'll throw a dagger into his gullet. I don't trust the bastard not to cheat."

The paunchy fourth man turned his gaze on Shaldon, a piercing silver challenge as sharp as the sword Payne-Elsdon was fondling. Their eyes locked in a contest of wills he was determined to win.

Step up, man. Step up. He'd waited these many years for the Duque de San Sebastian to step up.

"Let me shoot him, Father," Charles said. "Queasy as I am, I can make the shot."

The Duque de San Sebastian had once gravely insulted Charles's wife.

"That would be murder, and this is my fight," he said, keeping his eye on the Duque. "Nauseous, are you, Charles?"

"Queer as Dick's hatband and almost ready to cast up my kidneys."

"Penderbrook's green at the gills, also," Kincaid said, "and Shaw. The Major looks hale enough."

"He's a bull," Charles said, his voice thin.

"A long negotiation, then," Kincaid said.

Charles would collapse first, or pretend to, and then Penderbrook. Though Shaw looked ready to be the first to drop.

They would parley until the Major required a new second, until the Major's own dosing took effect. He and his man might ask to postpone the match to another day, but Shaldon would not allow it.

"Good luck, Father," Charles said. "I must go and throw up."

The silver gaze still bore into him and finally, the man's lips turned up in a sneer.

Shaw returned, blocking his view of the Duque. The Major's second swallowed hard, took some deep breaths, and handed back one of the small swords.

"We accept the weapon, with one demand. First blood will not suffice for satisfaction. It must be *à l'outrance*."

A fight to the death. "I expected no less," Shaldon said. "Yes. That would give me satisfaction also. Kincaid?"

"Aye, my lord?"

"Send men to the magistrate and the guard."

"Here now, Shaldon..." Shaw's voice tapered off, his color fading, his hand going to his mouth. He turned away, taking deep breaths.

The Major must have noticed his man's distress. He swaggered down from the heights, paler than he'd been at the musicale, his mouth grim.

"Good day, Major," Shaldon said. "Shaw has given me your terms. A fight to the death, so it will be. But I will apprise you of ours: since only a hot-headed fool or a cold-hearted murderer would require this sort of Continental blood sport—*à l'outrance*, indeed—that man, if he prevails, and," he nodded at Shaw, "the men who conspire with him, will submit to a trial for murder."

"He's sent a man for the magistrate," Shaw said.

"Has he?" the Major growled. "We'd best hurry and finish up. Call your groveling puppy over, Shaldon, and let's get on with it."

"Furthermore," Shaldon said, addressing Shaw, "if this murderous thug *doesn't* prevail, there will be no need for a trial, as his opponent may safely assert self-defense, based on his demand to kill. Now, Shaw, you're rather green. Cast up your accounts, if that's what you're planning, and let's talk about the rest of the rules of this fight. Major, you may go back to the sideline and bide your time, there's a good chap."

The Major's lip twisted, and color flooded his jaundiced cheeks, turning them a sickly orange. He'd carried out his murderous duels in France and Spain, but he'd never faced official consequences.

And he wouldn't now. The call for a magistrate was merely a fallback plan should the worst happen.

"Stop the nonsense, Shaldon. Bring your *boy* out. Now."

"We are not in France, nor Italy, nor Spain, Major. This is not battle, nor a street fight. You have accepted a gentleman's challenge, and you must allow the seconds to discuss the terms."

Shaw bent over and vomited.

"We'll start with the location." He eyed the ground at the other man's feet, "Not here. Let us move to the carriage path when you are finished spewing, Shaw."

. . .

JANE STOOD ASIDE FIDGETING WHILE GRACIELA CHATTERED through excited introductions. Graciela's father, Captain Kingsley, was lean and hard as a privateer must be, and it was obvious he'd suffered on some occasion, no doubt battling for his life. A scar marred his handsome jaw, and he favored one side when walking, the way Shaldon sometimes did.

She knew bits and pieces of Captain Kingsley's story, and she didn't have time for the rest of it. Shaldon was seconding her son in a duel.

She needed to stop them.

"Papa," Graciela said, "we must talk about Charley and little Reina later. For now, Lady Jane needs your help."

Tears sprang to Jane's eyes. *Bless the girl.*

Captain Kingsley's warm gaze fixed on her. "I'm at your service, my lady."

Her breath froze and she struggled to speak. "My son is…I've just learned…" She eased in a breath.

"They've just left for a duel," Graciela said.

"Shaldon is seconding," Sirena said.

"I must…I must go." Jane nodded to Jenny. "Where is it taking place?"

"I don't know, my lady."

"*Someone* must know." She drove a fist into her palm. "Ask the serv—"

"Battersea Fields." Lloyd hadn't left them. "My lady, perhaps Captain Kingsley could go on your behalf."

"No. I must go." She hurried to the door.

"Go, Papa." Graciela's tense voice rang clearly behind her. "You must help Lady Jane. And Charley is there. And if a melee breaks out, they may all need your sword arm."

She paused on the landing. A melee, with all of them involved. It was too wretchedly uncivilized to imagine.

Footsteps clattered behind her, following her down the stairs, out the door, and onto the street. Ewan waved her over to a plain black carriage, and one of Shaldon's coachmen saluted her. The boy helped her in and handed her the case.

"Where is Guignard?" she asked.

"Scampered when Lloyd sent the Earl's carriage around, my lady."

Ewan climbed in and pulled the door, meeting resistance.

"Wait." Jane touched the boy's arm. "Captain Kingsley is joining us."

Ewan sent him a measuring look, which the Captain ignored.

"Battersea Fields," Kingsley shouted. "In all haste."

As the wheels started to roll, the door jerked open again and Jenny clambered in, sending Ewan a glare and taking the rear-facing seat next to him while the coach clattered off.

"You'll need me my lady," she said.

She nodded, mutely. Perhaps Jenny was also good with a blade.

The Shaldon servants were a loyal bunch, starting with their butler. Lloyd, dear Lloyd, must have ordered this coach the moment he saw her race through the door. He'd have preferred to send Captain Kingsley in her place, but he'd expected her to want to go. Lloyd was loyal to her.

Did he know of Shaldon's proposal?

She mulled over the notion while they turned onto the main street. Horses moved past them on either side.

Outriders. Lloyd had arranged for them as well.

Lloyd, Shaldon's long-time butler wanted someone to

intervene, and he didn't mind if that someone was Lady Jane.

Captain Kingsley settled back on the seat next to her. "Now, will you tell me, my lady, what the devil is going on?"

The coach hit a bump and her heart lurched with it. Up ahead, the riders must be clearing the thoroughfare, as they were making good speed past raised fists and hurled curses.

She blinked back sudden moisture. She could lose her son today. Or...Shaldon. Dear Lord, she didn't want the man to die.

Jenny cleared her throat.

Jane sat up and handed the valise to the girl. "Open the tube, Jenny." She put a hand to her waist, drawing in a deep breath. "Captain Kingsley, yes. Yes, I will tell you. I have a son, Quentin Penderbrook, raised as a gentleman by a vicar and his wife. He was born out of wedlock when I was very, very young."

My son, my only child. She'd held him for mere moments, looking into dark blue eyes that had studied her back, and then he'd been whisked away so she could rest. When she'd awakened again, he was gone.

Swallowing hard, she went on. "He owed a great deal of money to a Major Payne-Elsdon, late of his majesty's service in Spain. Before I could attempt to assist him, Shaldon paid off the debt. Payne-Elsdon learned of my son's parentage and insulted both him and me in front of all the members of White's, provoking a challenge by the foolish boy. Shaldon forbade his sons from serving as his second. He is doing it himself."

"A concise report."

The Captain took her hand and squeezed it, the kind gesture making her eyes water more. *Devil take it.* She wiped a gloved hand across her cheeks.

"I thank you," he said affably.

"I've no idea if Quentin can use a sword."

"My lady," Jenny said. "There *is* something here."

CHAPTER TWENTY

"*P*ull it out," Jane said.

The girl eased out the canvas and handed it over to Jane.

Holding it up before her, she let it unroll.

Felicity and Perpetua looked imploringly up to heaven.

Captain Kingsley snorted. "I take it the Duque de San Sebastian is involved in this fight today?"

The Duque?

The Captain reached for the edge of the painting, tugging it straight, and she remembered. He'd taken the painting from the Duque many years ago.

"I called on him this morning," she said, "to sell him this. The Duquesa told me he went out to attend a duel."

"Might he be this major's second? Perhaps Shaldon will fight *him*."

"I don't see how. It will have to be my son and the Major."

Ewan cleared his throat. "Begging your pardon, my lady, but I don't believe his lordship means for your son to fight at all."

Ewen looked nervous. She'd been led to believe that the consummately professional Shaldon servants refrained from all gossip.

But Jenny was a Shaldon servant, and she had, somehow, through a network of gossips, heard all of the news from White's.

"For heaven's sake, boy, tell us," the Captain said.

"It's summat to do with the brandy, sir. One of Lord Bakeley's rare bottles. They opened it last night, then corked it again right away, like new, and after Mr. Penderbrook and Mr. Everly drank half the bottle this morning, they poured the rest out."

"You learned all of that while waiting outside for me?" Jane said.

Jenny gave the boy an appreciative look.

"Who are *they*?" Captain Kingsley asked.

Ewan bit his lip. "I don't know exactly, sir."

"*They*...dear God." Her heart lurched. "*Shaldon* and Kincaid poisoned them?"

"I don't know, my lady."

"Did Bakeley partake?" Kingsley asked.

"They say not sir."

"Shaldon?"

"No, sir. Only the two of them, Mr. Penderbrook and Mr. Everly."

"Well." Kingsley shook his head. "And I thought I'd find London dull." He chuckled. "Do not worry, my lady, if Shaldon dosed his own son, I don't imagine the potion will be fatal to yours. Graciela must not know I'm meeting my new son-in-law for the first time in a bad state, else she wouldn't have encouraged me to come. What will it be, do you think? Casting up their accounts, the flux, or the sleep of the poppy?"

"Not the poppy." Not after Shaldon's drugging in Yorkshire. It had taken him days to shake off the effects of the laudanum.

She thought about his renewed offer of marriage—perhaps he still hadn't shaken the full effects.

The Captain nodded. "Well, in any case, no matter the poison, Shaldon means for it to come down to a fight between the Duque and himself."

Her heart skipped a beat. Shaldon would fight? Might be fighting right now, this moment?

"He can't. He was wounded less than a fortnight ago," she said, breathless. "He hasn't completely healed." The foolish man, why would he do this?

For you, her heart whispered, and she turned to look out the window, blinking.

That couldn't be. She'd seen him kissing the Duquesa. This was not for her, this was for him, for the opportunity to get revenge.

But if he died, what then? The infuriating man would cease to plague her, and she couldn't bear it. And what if, by some miracle—or curse—she was with child again, even at her advanced age?

She struggled for a breath and looked up into Jenny's concerned gaze.

"Sir," Jenny said, "Is his lordship any good with a sword?"

"Shaldon?" The Captain glanced at Jane and quickly patted her hand. "The Shaldon I know? Never fear, my lady, he *will* find a way. What Shaldon wants, Shaldon gets."

"Dear God," she whispered. "Can we go any faster?"

"If Mr. Penderbrook is to fight, we will need to postpone, my lord." Russell, the surgeon Kincaid had engaged, cast a glance back at Charles and Penderbrook. Both were bent over the side of the carriage path, retching and holding their bellies, ready to keel over.

"I agree." Payne-Elsdon's surgeon hooked a finger toward the other side, where Shaw was gagging into a soggy handkerchief. "It's a certainty that it would be no fair fight for either your principal or the Major's second."

The Major broke off from a huddle with the Duque and marched over to the three men.

"Mr. Penderbrook cannot fight," the Major's medical man said. "Nor can Mr. Shaw."

Payne-Elsdon's eyes narrowed tensely. His face had gone paler, his lips grayer. "What the devil is this, Shaldon? What have you done?"

"Are you well, Major?" Shaldon asked. "You're looking a bit green yourself."

The Duque stepped up to join them. "Three men who take part in a duel today become ill? What English illness is this?"

"Perhaps it was something served up at White's?" Shaldon flicked a stray leaf from his black shirt. The wind had picked up, with clouds blowing in. "Did you all visit the club last night?"

"There is also an influenza being talked of," Russell said.

"Shaldon fever, more likely," the Major said. "You've poisoned my second." His eyes glazed and a sheen of perspiration appeared on his brow.

Very, very good. They might soon finish this tedious negotiating. "Poisoned, Major? A strong word."

The Major pulled a handkerchief and mopped at his brow. "What sort of honorable man cheats at a duel?"

"You are calling *me* a cheat because Shaw ate some fouled clams? Look over there—Penderbrook and *my son* are both retching. If three men..." and very soon, he hoped, four... "should become ill at the same time, how is that cheating?"

"You know very well." He winced, and his hand went to his belly.

"Fine. We can simply proceed, Major, you and I."

"Perhaps, in that case, a match with pistols is a better choice," the Major's surgeon said.

"*Pistols?*" Shaldon infused the word with contempt. "In our negotiations, Shaw was unbending. No, after so much obduracy and aggravation, we will proceed with the sword."

"But my lord," the Major's surgeon said. "A man of your age—"

"*Of my age?* Oh ho, or are you worried your man here is flagging? I observe that you are not looking well, Major."

"You must postpone," the surgeon insisted.

Heat came over him, and he pushed it down reminding himself that anger could cast a pall over a man's ability to think. "We will not."

The silver eyes pinned him yet again, and he stared back, shielding the ire threatening to boil over. "This nonsense has occupied too much of my time already. Perhaps you may choose another second, Major. A man of my age, eh? The Duque, here, is a notable swordsman, or so I have heard from his enemies who fought on the side of the people of Spain."

A flare of temper lit the Duque's eyes.

"You're a fraud, Shaldon." Sweating, looking ready to faint, the Major drew the sword from its sheath, brandishing it. "A cheater in a question of honor."

A rustle next to him signaled Kincaid's presence. His pistol would be ready, should the major wave that sharp tip any closer.

"Whose honor, Major? Oh yes, I remember—Penderbrook's, and Lady Jane's. And mine. As for your honor—well." He nodded. "It is common knowledge that you have none."

A red haze came over the man.

"No need to go into a snit. I know all about the young men you bully-cocked into duels on the Continent and the Peninsula. One or two sons of some very powerful men, which is why I believe you made your way to England."

Yet another coach was waiting beyond the trees to see to those offenses. Good that the Major would soon be incapacitated by the concoction of herbs.

"And your expertise at cards? It's whispered about quite openly at White's what a cunning shaver you are. And then there's your *service* in the Peninsula. What a real bravo you were there, double-dealing with the French and the *afrancesados*."

The Major lunged, and Shaldon jumped back just in time, the tip almost grazing him. A fat bejeweled hand seized the other man's arm.

"There's a gun pointed at you, you fool," the Duque said.

Kincaid had drawn his pistol.

"You see?" Shaldon said. "Attacking an unarmed man. What say you, surgeon? Can your man fight, or not?"

"Draw the damn sword, you churl, and let's finish this," Payne-Elsdon said. Then he doubled over and spewed.

Shaldon raised an eyebrow and turned his gaze on the Duque. "Yes," he said. "Let's finish this."

The Duque's lip curled, and he removed his hat, tossing it to his servant.

Shaldon pulled off his coat and murmured to Kincaid, "Get Penderbrook out of here before the magistrate arrives."

. . .

WHEN THEY REACHED THE RICKETY BATTERSEA BRIDGE, THE driver slowed. Jane clung to the window's edge and peered out, but she could see nothing blocking them.

Captain Kingsley craned his head out the other window. "They haven't yet torn this bridge down?"

"Vauxhall would be the safer crossing, but it's out of the way," Ewan said. "This is faster."

"Providing we make it across," the Captain said.

Across the Thames, Battersea Fields stood, a long stretch of green dotted with trees, and no one in sight. Somewhere hiding in there, her son or Shaldon might be fighting right now for her honor—and his life. And if either died, would *her* life be worth anything?

She shoved down the thought. Damn it, in spite of his affair with the Duquesa she didn't want Shaldon dead. Neither man could die. She, somehow, would not allow it. She'd lost too many men in her life already.

"How can we possibly find them?" she asked.

"Beyond the Pigeon Shooting Grounds," Ewan said. "John Coachman will know the way."

"I know the place," Captain Kingsley said. "A dry stretch there beyond a marsh. Had occasion to visit Battersea myself, though it's been an age."

It would be an age crossing the bridge if they did not go on faster. The carriage came to a complete halt, and Ewan jumped out to check.

"We should walk." Jane started to rise, but the Captain touched her arm.

"Patience, my lady. Once we cross, we will make great haste."

Ewan popped back in. "The riders are clearing the

bridge. We must wait for a market cart that is halfway across, else we may not be able to pass."

She forced herself to lean back against the squab. Patience? She was deadly sick of summoning her patience, completely dry of it.

She rubbed a thumb over the soft seat. This was another Shaldon coach, discreetly elegant with velvet upholstery and good padding underneath.

If she could but have a second chance, if she could wean the Earl away from his dallying, this could be hers.

Could have been hers. She'd seen the Major at the musicale—given the opportunity, the Major would kill.

No. Shaldon was no wilting fern. He was a tall, strong, active man, a hard man.

But his opponent was built like a bull. And he was many years younger.

She gripped her hands and looked out the window, watching the play of the wind on the river. Clouds were moving in, dark and filled with angry moisture.

It had rained the night Reginald and her brother died. It had rained the night before their death, the night when Shaldon appeared at their home to join them for dinner. Father had not been happy to set the extra place at table, but one did not refuse hospitality to a powerful earl.

Shaldon had been gracious and reserved that night. He had spoken to her, a mere young girl. He had noticed her, politely, distantly, and she had noticed him, the way one notices a handsome, older, unattainable man one has no interest in.

And she'd been jealous. When Shaldon beckoned, Reginald went, and her brother also, in the way of men everywhere. Men's men, they were, and the ladies could be satisfied with the crumbs of attention cast their way.

"And there's the cart, my lady."

Ewen's voice ripped her back from her dark memories. The wide country cart passed and their coach began to move, crawling across the decrepit wooden bridge. They turned down a carriage path and stopped again.

"What is it this time?" Jane asked.

"I'll check." Ewan jumped out, and the Captain followed him. Moments later, they moved forward, pulling to the side, and another coach passed.

Captain Kingsley pushed Charley Everly in and climbed in behind him.

CHAPTER TWENTY-ONE

*C*harley clutched a carriage blanket before him and managed a grin with his greeting.

"Better sit facing forward," the Captain said, placing Charley next to Jane and taking the seat next to Jenny.

"You are ill," Jane said. "Where is…"

"Penderbrook? In that carriage. Best he be off before the guard arrives."

"The guard?" she asked, stupidly.

Captain Kingsley extended a flask, but Charley waved it away.

"The Horse Guard. And a magistrate. Duels are illegal."

"Dear God," she muttered. "Is he truly ill?" She craned her head to look out the window. Her son would be mortified, to issue a challenge and be too weak to follow through.

But *she* was relieved. She'd rather have him branded a coward—even if he hated her forever—than die so foolishly.

"This will pass." Charley pressed the blanket to his mouth. "You will see your son shortly. Father has everything in hand."

"I sent your groom along with him," Kingsley said. "Has the duel started?"

"Probably. Father was tossing off his coats when Kincaid hustled us out."

Her head was spinning, trying to keep up. Shaldon had sent them away. The duel was starting. The guard was coming. They would arrest him.

But no, of course not. They wouldn't arrest the Earl of Shaldon.

"Who is he fighting?" Jane asked. "The Major?"

Charley shook his head, grimacing before commencing a fit of dry heaving.

She held his shaking shoulders, while Kingsley looked on, a glint of amusement in his eyes.

To find Charley's illness diverting, the Captain must be another man of the Shaldon ilk.

"He poisoned your brandy," she said.

Charley nodded.

"Your father is mad."

His spasms ending, Charley waved a hand. "I volunteered, my lady," he said on a tight breath. "It was the only way he'd allow me to help Pender and you."

Kingsley pressed the flask into the younger man's hand. "I wondered what sort of man Graciela would settle on. Take a swig, Everly."

RID OF HIS COATS, SHALDON RAISED THE BLADE IN A SALUTE, one his opponent, the vile, grasping villain, didn't deserve.

The Duque didn't deserve a gentleman's fight, and he damned well wouldn't get one today.

They circled around on the bumpy ground. The Duque's paunch was a fair target, though too padded for a lethal poke. That layer of fat might be useful though in keeping the Duque off balance. He'd been a formidable fighter when younger, or so it was said. Shaldon had seen naught but the man's command of his bullies.

The Duque opened, and Shaldon thrust, coming up short as the man jumped back, and feeling the slice of the blade on his own arm.

He pulled back. The stroke had burned, but the muscle in that arm worked, and he daren't look at the cut.

The Duque slashed. He parried, shoved the man off balance, and lunged. When he retreated, the Duque's white shirt sported a crimson line.

He attacked then with a flurry of thrusts and parries, the other man answering as if he hadn't been touched.

When the Duque's blade pierced his shoulder, he tripped and fell back.

CRAWLING OVER THE BUMPY ROAD, THE CARRIAGE CAME around a bend.

Jane craned her head out the window and spotted them.

Shaldon was stripped down to a black shirt and trousers, his sword whizzing and clashing with that of the Duque in his white frills.

She shoved the rolled canvas under her arm, kicked open the door, and jumped out.

A large body blocked her.

"*You,*" Jenny cried.

Kincaid's Scotsman glanced over Jane's shoulder and his face lit.

Jenny shoved to the front. "Move out of the way, *right now*, Fergus MacEwen."

Jane darted around the hulking man and spotted Bakeley and Kincaid standing a short distance from the battle.

Her vision tunneled on the pistol in Bakeley's hand. Neither man saw her.

She hurried up, wrenched the gun away, and ran.

The frenzy increased, blades flashing and clanging, the wild thrusting and parrying accelerating. They didn't see her.

"Stop," she cried. A hand gripped her elbow and pulled her out of the way of the Duque's wild swing. Shaldon attacked, and the Duque dodged and came around thrusting. His sword came back bloody, and Shaldon fell, scrabbling away on his bottom.

The villain drew back his arm with a tight smile.

"*Stop.*" She shook off the hand grasping her and stumbled between the men, raising the pistol.

Rocks clattered behind her. "Jane—"

"Look here, Duque." Shaldon could wait. She held up the canvas and waved it.

The Duque's eyes widened and then narrowed on something over her shoulder.

"I'm all right Jane," Shaldon murmured into her ear. "Kindly move out of the way. I fear you are in danger."

"*No.*" She took a deep breath.

"You *should* move, madam," the Duque said. "His lordship is attempting to recover your honor."

The blackguard. The villain. The traitorous pig.

She took another breath. The pistol was heavy. Her gun hand was shaking.

The weapon was not needed, was it? They'd stopped, hadn't they?

Not even she would commit murder on her own

account this day. No one would die. Too many men had died. She would see this to a peaceful conclusion, whether Shaldon liked it or not.

"What utter rubbish you talk, Duque," she said. "My honor is completely intact, with or without this fighting. *Now*. I have something here that you want." Fumbling one-handed with the canvas, she let it unroll.

The Duque froze, his gaze fixed on the dark image.

"I am taking bids," she said.

"Bids?" the Duque's lip curled. He reached for the canvas and she yanked it away.

"It is mine." He growled and raised his blade. She stumbled, the blade whizzed, and the pistol exploded, knocking her back into a hard chest.

The Duque howled, oaths pouring from him. A deep burn flared in her shoulder and gunpowder filled her nose.

Had she somehow shot herself? Vision clouding, she wilted, and her feet gave completely away.

"*Jane.*"

Panic flared in him. *Not Jane.*

Shaldon caught her against him as she sank to the ground, ignoring the bustle of action around him as others rushed in.

A spot was growing in the dark shoulder of her pelisse, a spot darker than the brown she'd so prudently worn. Like him, she'd dressed for battle, the foolish, brave, dear girl.

"Russell," he yelled.

"Here, my lord."

He gathered her and started to lift, but pain tore at his own shoulder.

"Let me, Father."

That voice was Bakeley's.

"I can walk," Jane said, and she proved it by getting to her feet. "Am I shot?"

"No," he said. "I do believe the ball hit the Duque."

The Duque's surgeon and servant supported the fat lout as he settled onto the nearby ground, swearing.

She gripped his hand, her breath feathering his ear. "*No.* Have I k-killed him?"

"Not the way he's caterwauling," Kincaid said.

"His foot seems to be bleeding, my lady," Bakeley said.

Jane's good arm found his own uninjured one, and they wobbled together.

Someone had laid out a quilt, and Russell was opening his case, the maid at his elbow, and behind her, MacEwen.

The clatter of horses drew Bakeley away. The guard had arrived.

Jane watched them dismount, clutching his arm. "Will they arrest us?"

His heart swelled, wiping out the throbbing in his various wounds. *Us,* she'd said. She was in this with him, though he doubted she'd thank him much if they ended up facing a magistrate together.

He helped her to the ground and pulled the string on her bonnet, wrenching it out of the way. "They'll be looking for the duel between Quentin Penderbrook and Major Payne-Elsdon, and neither of them are here. This was a mere bit of sword practice between two old survivors of the wars in the Peninsula."

"They will have heard the pistol shot." She gripped his hand. "What will I say?"

"You won't have to talk to them. I'll see to it."

Russell handed the maid a pair of shears and she nudged

in between them and began cutting away the shoulder of Jane's gown.

"Let's have a look at you, my lord." Shaldon let the surgeon rip away his black shirt, wincing as the man probed, watching as Jane's wound was revealed. A gash ran across the top of her arm.

"Take care of her first," Shaldon said.

Russell glanced over at her. "Press a clean cloth to that wound," he told the maid. "Now, you, my lord, have a puncture wound here." He pressed an ear to Shaldon's chest. "No wheezing in the lungs. And there are a few cuts we'll tend to directly." He waved at MacEwen. "Find his coats." He went to Jane's side and began to examine her.

JANE WATCHED SHALDON, HIS TORN SHIRT HANGING OPEN, deal with the guard captain and the magistrate who had appeared, barely hearing the conversation. The Duque had finally stopped squawking. In the crush and commotion she couldn't see the man.

Would he die of that wound? She hadn't meant to shoot him. It had been accidental, a mere reaction to his blow.

She'd never have believed it possible that a gentleman would strike a lady like that.

At least Quentin had got away, and they were all, at least for now, alive.

They were *alive*.

When the surgeon finished with her, Jenny draped a blanket over her and helped her up. MacEwen joined them and escorted her to the carriage.

"What of Lord Shaldon?" she asked.

"His lordship will be right along," MacEwen said.

The shooting was her crime, not his. "I should go and join him—"

"My lady," MacEwen said, "he's spinning a tale to the magistrate about how a Spanish duke happened to be shot during their sword practice. Best let him handle it. He'll join you directly."

"He's right, Lady Jane," Jenny said, glaring at MacEwen, "this time."

CHAPTER TWENTY-TWO

*J*ane gazed up at the canopy overhanging the bed. The drop of laudanum the surgeon had pushed on her had made her woozy. The details of her arrival here were equally unclear, but she knew they'd been heading to Shaldon House.

Lady Sirena hovered nearby, and Lady Perry gazed at her from the foot of the bed.

"Has Shaldon arrived yet?" she asked.

"Not yet," Sirena said. "Nor Bakeley. Charley is back, though, and Gracie is tending to him."

"Quentin?"

"In a guest chamber moaning and heaving. The surgeon's man looked in on both him and Charley after he sewed you up. One of the footmen is with him now."

She lifted her head and looked around. This wasn't her old room at Shaldon House, but another bedchamber, decorated in spring greens and with silky curtains; a feminine room.

She sat up and pain stabbed her. She'd refused more

laudanum, wanting her wits about her for what was to come, whatever that might be.

And how was she to deal with Shaldon? For all she knew, he'd been taken up by the authorities, all for protecting her honor and her son's.

And managing his feud with the Duque too, she must not forget that.

Her stomach roiled. She'd shot a Spanish nobleman. The Duque's wound could fester. He could lose his foot. He could lose his leg. He could die, and she'd be his murderer.

Lady Perry came around the bed. "Let me help you, Lady Jane. Remember how many times you scolded Kincaid about ripping his stitches?" The younger woman slipped an arm under her, helping her to sit up fully and swing her legs off the bed. "You must be mindful of your injury. But what excitement you've had, taking part in a duel."

Sirena laughed. "After filching his lordship's painting right under his nose." She waggled a finger. "And not letting us in on the secret."

The painting. Oh, blast it. "I left the painting there."

"Father will see it comes home," Perry said.

"That was a copy. Shaldon already has the original."

Sirena laughed out loud. "Of course, he does. You must tell us everything."

"Almost everything," Perry said with a sly grin.

Heat rose in Jane, pounding through all of her aching muscles into her cheeks. They knew about her night with Shaldon. *How*, she didn't know.

"Do I have clothing here? I want to be dressed when the men return." And when Quentin was recovered enough to talk. "Help me into a gown and I'll tell you almost everything."

"But we just managed to get you into the nightgown, and the surgeon said—"

"It is only a deep cut. My arm is still intact, my hands and fingers work, and I want to dress. I must speak with your father, and I'm not going to entertain him in any part of this house wearing a nightgown." Especially one as filmy and revealing as the one they'd dressed her in. "If he is too ill to come downstairs, once I am fully clothed I'll go along to his bedchamber."

Sirena and Perry exchanged a glance. "You won't have far to go, Jane." Sirena walked to a door and opened it.

Jane stumbled to the doorway on Perry's arm. The room beyond held a grand bed with rich dark blue hangings. Books and papers littered a table, and a massive wing chair sat near the fireplace, a padded hassock bumped up against it.

Her pulse quickened, her wound picking up its throbbing, and she remembered: the bed she'd shared with Perry at Gorse Point Cottage had been Lady Shaldon's, hung with the same green-patterned cloth.

"You put me in your mother's room?" She pressed Perry's arm. "How could you?"

She must get out of here.

"Call us hopeful," Sirena said.

Perry squeezed her free hand. "And, if you but allow it, we will call you *Mother*."

As she spoke, the corridor door to the other chamber opened and Shaldon entered, supported by Kincaid and Bakeley, the surgeon who'd tended her wounds trailing behind, and Lloyd following with the surgeon's bag.

Shaldon glanced her way and their gazes locked.

His lips turned up in a boyish grin, sending her heart pounding harder. Heat tingled through her, making her conscious of her dishabille, and the long plait of hair that hung over her shoulder.

She stepped back and closed the door. There was no lock, no key. Apparently, the Earls of Shaldon had full access to their lady wives.

But she was not Lady Shaldon, and she must leave this bedchamber directly.

There was no time for the complicated business of stays, gown and coiffure. "Find me a dressing gown, at once, Sirena. Perry, gather my things. I am not staying here."

"Lloyd, find me a banyan."

"Let Russell tend you first, Father," Bakeley said.

He lurched toward the wardrobe, but Kincaid interceded, finding the blasted dressing gown and helping him into it.

"I must talk to Jane."

"Getting ready to bolt again, is she?" Kincaid muttered.

"Father—"

"Bakeley, come with me and chase your wife and your sister out. Lloyd, go and tell Cook to send a tray up to Lady Jane's bedchamber. Take Russell with you and feed him."

"But, Father—"

"It's all right, Bakeley," Kincaid said. "Russell treated his lordship's stab wound on the field, and the cuts are small enough to keep for now."

Bakeley took his arm, but he shook it off and straightened, ignoring a flare of pain. He would walk through that damn door on his own.

He pushed it open. Perry looked up from the dressing table and grinned. Sirena craned her head from the clothes press, where she was poking around.

Lady Jane clutched a bed hanging and pulled it in front of her. "Shaldon," she squeaked. "What—oh, blast it, why am I surprised? You need to leave this moment, sir."

Bakeley went to his lady, who had finally found what she was looking for, a filmy feminine robe. He yanked the garment from his wife and tossed it. Shaldon caught it, pain shooting through his shoulder.

"You fool man." Lady Jane must have seen him wince. "Let the surgeon see to those wounds."

"Everyone out," he said. "Except you, Jane. I must beg an audience." He moved nearer and draped the dressing gown over her shoulders. Behind them, one of the girls giggled and the door latch clicked.

She leaned her forehead against the bedpost. "They are as insufferable as you, Shaldon."

He'd been counting on that.

"I'm not sleeping in your wife's bedchamber."

When she stood tall, the loose braid settled along the length of her proud back. "Can you manage getting your arm into this sleeve?" he asked.

He paused, catching a breath. The bandage showed white under the thin lawn and lace of her gown. One more thing to settle with the Duque de San Sebastian.

"I was hoping you would be willing to sleep in *my* bedchamber. And I'm so sorry the Duque struck you, the cur."

She extended her arm and allowed his help, accepting the braid as he passed it over her shoulder. He'd wedged his amorous hopes between helpfulness and apologies, and she hadn't noticed.

When she turned to him, her eyes were clouded with anguish.

Dammit, why had he mentioned the cursed Duque at all?

"Will he die, do you think?"

"He may lose a toe, an insignificant appendage, but with good care, there should be no infection. His boot partially shielded him." He paused, pushing back at the anger rising in him. "It will teach him not to abuse a strong lady."

She nodded. "What of the Major?" She clutched her hands at her waist.

"The Major will not plague you or Penderbrook ever again."

"How can you be so sure?"

"There was a yacht waiting for him in the Pool. He's on his way to Spain."

"*He escaped?*" She cried.

He reached for her hand. "No. He is in the custody of a powerful Spaniard whose son he killed in a duel."

"Oh." Her head whirled with the news. How could a woman ever hope to keep up with a man like this? She swallowed hard and searched his face for deception, finding none.

"His captor is a friend of the Duquesa's father."

"Oh. You...you discussed this in one of your liaisons with her?"

"Yes." He paused, his gaze thoughtful. "But no—they were never liaisons. She is an ally, not a lover."

And now she knew he was lying. She pulled her hand out of his grasp.

"I *saw* you with her, with my own eyes."

He blinked.

That was all. One did not catch the Spy Lord often in one of his lies, and of course, he was unlikely to confirm or deny the truth of her assertion.

But she would get the truth, about the Duquesa, about the duel, about her son's poisoning, about everything that had happened that day, and then she would gather her things and leave. Like Jenny, she had no use for a faithless man.

"Do you kiss all your allies with such passion?"

He swiped a hand over his face. "Jane—"

"None of your lies, Shaldon."

"But, Jane—"

"You may make love to whatever allies you wish. I am not sleeping in your bed, *or* your late wife's. I am going home."

Home. As soon as the word left her mouth her heart fell. She had no true home, only a dilapidated cottage in Ireland she couldn't afford to repair.

But she would find a home. She would return to Gerrard Street for the time being until she could arrange other lodgings.

A knock at the door brought servants with trays, giving her time before she needed to say more, before *he* could plague her again.

As the servants left, another figure slipped in, pale-faced, hair in disarray, but otherwise perfectly dressed and groomed.

She went to him.

He bowed and said, "Mother."

The cascade of emotions on his face, the pasty color, they had nothing to do with his illness—his poisoning. This was abject misery.

"I heard you were injured. I'm sorry, Mother. I meant to defend your honor and I failed."

"Please, my dear," she said, "come and sit down." Only

two chairs graced the table. She should eject Shaldon from the room.

"Penderbrook," Shaldon said, "fetch the extra chair from the dressing table. Come, my lady." He took her elbow and steered her to her seat.

Quentin shook his head. "I will stand. I came only to say goodbye." He bit his lip. "I must leave England. I am ruined."

CHAPTER TWENTY-THREE

"*R*uined?"

Her vision clouded and she gripped the table edge, leaning in, struggling for a breath. "*You're leaving England? You're ruined?*" The damned fool. "As if you have any idea what it is to be ruined." She unclenched her hands, straightened, and jabbed a finger at him. "You will carry that chair over. You will sit down and join us. Lord Shaldon has things he must tell us about today."

His brows pinched together and his mouth firmed into a hard line.

"*Quentin*, there are things you and I *must* hear."

He bit down on his lip, but fetched the chair.

What kind of mother might she have been to a strong-willed boy? Regret poked at her, and she pushed it aside. She must help her pigheaded son find the good sense that should be his legacy from her.

She *was* sensible, mostly.

Shaldon seated her and then himself, and only then would Quentin sit. The Earl's face was a cypher, but Quentin's demeanor screamed obstinance.

Blasted men. She looked hard at Shaldon, nodded her head toward her son, and cleared her throat. "My lord?"

"Charles will go with you to White's tomorrow, Penderbrook," he said, "where you will learn that other members of the club succumbed to a severe dyspepsia."

Quentin's shoulders lifted.

Jane handed Shaldon his tea. "You sir, are a devious one." She poured another cup and heaped in sugar. "Drink this," she said, handing the cup to Quentin, "it will help settle your stomach and get your strength back."

He grimaced and took a sip. "Nevertheless, I'm doomed when the Major comes into White's."

"He won't return to White's," Shaldon said.

His head came up from the cup. "He'll be expelled?"

"What he did was not the act of an honorable man, not even if he'd been completely befuddled with drink. But he won't return to White's because he won't return to England."

"His past has caught up with him," Jane said.

As hers had caught up with her. She hadn't chased after the past, the way Shaldon had. She'd simply deferred her day of reckoning.

Perhaps Shaldon's way was better. He didn't hide from trouble. He addressed it head on.

She blinked and reached for a biscuit, nibbling without tasting, needing to keep her hands busy, as Shaldon recounted the Major's fate.

Quentin listened until the end and frowned. "The fellows will puzzle out that it was a fraud. I'm a fraud. They will laugh when they learn that my mother appeared and—"

"Damn the fellows," she cried, rising, and quickly seating herself again as he shot to his feet. "*Sit down*, Quentin."

"Mother, the Major can't just sail off for some rough Spanish justice. He attacked a lady. He cut you."

Quentin knew of her wound but hadn't been told who inflicted it. She glanced at Shaldon and he lifted an eyebrow.

"The Major had been poisoned as well," she said. "He didn't duel today."

"But Shaw was as ill as I. Too ill to—"

"Shaw didn't fight, either," she said. "It was the Duque who stepped in for the Major."

Shaldon rubbed his injured shoulder. "And got the better of me, I'm embarrassed to say. Your mother avenged me by shooting him."

Quentin turned wide eyes on her, as if he were really seeing her for the first time, a woman capable of shooting a Spanish nobleman. Perhaps from time to time effective mothering required such decisive violence.

She waved a hand. "Merely an accident."

"When he slashed her with his sword, she shot off his toe."

She lifted her cup but saw that her hand was shaking too much to drink from it. Settling it into the saucer, she drew in a deep breath. "You must write Mr. Walker and ask him to offer prayers that the Duque's wound doesn't fester. Much as I despise the grief the Duque caused..." She glanced at Shaldon. Given the scars on his body, he had suffered the most. "I don't want to take any man's life."

Quentin nodded, his mouth still agape. "May I also tell him about you, my lady?"

"Yes. And I shall pay him a visit soon, if he is willing to receive me."

He pushed back his chair. "I am feeling well enough to

excuse myself and return to my lodging. I've intruded on your hospitality too long, my lord."

"Penderbrook," Shaldon said. "Before you make your way to White's tomorrow, call on Bakeley. He has need of a new steward at his estate in Kent. He would like you to consider the position. It will take you from London, but you will need to visit often for business and to see Lady Jane, and when you do, you will stay here at Shaldon House. It will be more convenient for both of you."

Her breath caught. He was implying that she would still be living here. She must set him straight.

"Th-thank you, my lord."

Jane took the younger man's hand. "When you are finished with Bakeley tomorrow, come and see me in Gerrard Street."

"Gerrard Street?" Quentin looked from her to Shaldon and back again.

"Lady Hackwell is allowing me use of her home there." She walked with him to the door. "Thank you for defending my honor."

"I didn't—"

"Yes, you did. And you would have certainly been killed had Lord Shaldon not intervened. I am glad you were not."

He frowned down at her. "You should not have come out today, Mother. It's not done."

Bully her, would he?

She glanced over at Shaldon. Would he chastise her also?

"I'm not some helpless female," she said.

"Listen to your mother, Penderbrook," Shaldon said. "She's not a bit helpless. You'll find most women aren't."

He nodded to her, and sudden heat bolted through her, magnetic, overpowering. She whipped her gaze back to the young man in front of her, beating back sudden moisture. Shaldon would see that all went well for her son. He would take care of Quentin, and herself if she would allow it.

"Thank you, Mother." Quentin lifted her hand, kissed it, and slipped out.

She wrapped her arms at her waist and felt the pulling of the stitches and the weight of the wound. When a hand firmed under her elbow, she leaned into it.

THE DOOR CLOSED ON PENDERBROOK, AND SHALDON DREW her close.

She gasped.

"Damn it, I've hurt you." He gentled his touch.

"I'm fine."

"We're a pair, aren't we? Between the two of us we'll have but two able arms for the next few days." In truth, his own shoulder was beginning to throb more. He led her back to the chair. "I have more I must say. We are not finished. Can you manage the teapot?"

She frowned but obliged him, filling a cup. When she lifted her gaze to his, color had risen in her cheeks. Wisps of hair framed her face and her eyes had turned midnight blue.

She was not finding her way back to Gerrard Street. He would not allow it.

But...but if he must let her go, he would, if what he had to say drove her away.

His wife had chosen to gamble his life for a painting, but theirs had been a marriage arranged for the good of both families. By God, with Jane they would marry for his own good and hers, and they would start out with the greatest risk of all—honesty.

They would start with that in a moment. He filled a

small plate with slices of bread, beef, and cheese for each of them. "An ample repast. Do have some."

"What do you wish to tell me?"

She'd pursed her lips and straightened her back, and the challenge excited him. Not a compliant woman after all, but he hoped she would be a forgiving one.

"Let us eat, and then we'll talk. I'm in need of sustenance." Or he must be. It couldn't be entirely a falsehood—he hadn't eaten much since the night before. "Forgive my manners." He folded the bread in half and took a bite, and the warm loaf and savory meat did indeed rouse his appetite.

Her face softened as he'd hoped it would and she took a mouthful, and then another.

When he'd finished, she pushed aside her plate. She'd been eating by rote also.

He tugged at her braid and she brought her hand down over his. Slender and small, her hand was all softness like the rest of her.

Softness wrapped around a strong core, that was Jane. He should carry her to his bed and ravish her again. And he would do so, as soon as their wounds had healed and he had secured her agreement.

"I don't know what skills you employed or what fates came together for you to see my meeting with the Duquesa last night, but I will tell you the entire truth. I met her to make arrangements for Payne-Elsdon's undoing, and yes, I accepted a kiss from her. The Duquesa bestows passionate embraces on every Englishman she meets clandestinely, in the hope of being seen by one of her husband's spies. She claims to have no relations with her husband and takes every chance to goad him. The Duquesa is a beautiful woman, but I was not aroused, my dear."

"She purposely risks putting men in the way of a challenge?"

"She doesn't see it that way, and truly, there is no danger. Her passion is only for her father's political cause and the Duque knows it. Besides, since his French friends were driven from Spain, the Duque usually lets other men lift his sword for him." His thumb swept across the back of her hand. "Jane, she is not my lover. I have no other lovers but you."

She tilted her head, studying him, clearly skeptical. "She is a cool one. And if she made Payne-Elsdon disappear... well, that is a kindness. I almost believe you."

She tried to pull away, but he held on.

"Believe me, because it's the truth, and I want the truth between us, Jane. I'm asking you for your hand again. Both your hands. All of you. Claim this bedchamber and make it your own, as Lady Shaldon." He kissed her palm. "But before you say, 'Yes, of course I will marry you, Ned,' there's something else. I must tell you what happened the night your brother died. I didn't kill him, but the blame is mine."

CHAPTER TWENTY-FOUR

he blame is mine.

She held her breath and let the words sink in. He blamed himself for her brother's death?

At first, her father had raged on about Shaldon, because Shaldon was there, because Reginald was working for him.

But before he died, Father had laid the blame squarely where it belonged. Her brother's death had been her fault entirely.

Shaldon had claimed his guilt matter-of-factly, but that vein pulsed in his temple and his eyes glowed, as they had two nights ago when he'd come to her bedchamber. She knew he was as unsettled as she was.

And she couldn't have him carrying this guilt, this man who must carry the responsibility of so many hard choices.

She clasped his hand, struggling for breath. Shaldon would have all her secrets tonight. Let him do with them what he wanted. "You are wrong of course."

"I am not wrong, Jane. I'd followed a man to Kent. A spy, who'd been gathering information on our fortifications.

The French were plotting their invasion. In fact, they'd landed a small force in Wales under an American colonel."

"I remember that. Father was very worried about his estate."

"With good reason." He paused, probably choosing his words carefully even though the war was long over and there were no more armies with secret invasion plans.

"You may also recall that a mill had been planned in the area, two heavyweights with a great following of gentlemen attending. Worrisome in itself to have so many peers on the coast, and perfect cover for our man to meet his contact arriving there. Reginald Dempsey was one of my newer men, too green, too inexperienced, but I used him because he secured the invitation to stay with your family. He spent part of his visit scouting the coast. His task that night was to help follow the mark and see who he met with. No one expected your brother to be there."

She swallowed a lump. "Father forbade my brother from going. He didn't approve of the sport."

"When your brother appeared, they both plagued me to allow him to stay. I should have sent him out of harm's way, but I didn't."

She felt her chest squeezing. Shaldon didn't know the truth.

He shook his head. "I lost sight of the man we were following, and I lost sight of Dempsey and your brother."

She squeezed his hand, grateful to know the details Father had never shared.

"Dempsey ran off following him to the cliffs, his only back-up your brother. A boat below had brought in the man's French contact. Dempsey, the fool, didn't wait for the rest of us. He confronted them and your brother joined in."

She squeezed her eyes shut. She could imagine it—Amsden, who'd always been ready to step up and fight.

His death had been far more honorable than what her father had led her to believe, that he'd been brought down in a drunken brawl.

Had father known the truth? He must have, if he'd found fault with Shaldon.

"Thank you," she whispered.

"Thank me? I failed your brother, and Dempsey, and you. Had I known about you and Dempsey, Jane, had Dempsey lived. I would have made him—"

"Made him what? Marry me?" She shook her head. Marriage to Dempsey would have been appalling. She knew that now. "He would have made a dreadful husband. I don't believe my dowry would have been enough for him. He left debts, even in the village." Her father had been so angry about that too. "I'm thanking you because my father would not say what happened."

"We couldn't tell him the details. Very likely he suspected enough to curse me."

"Yes, there were some curses hurled your way." She choked and turned away. "In any case, he didn't blame you entirely. He mostly blamed me."

"You?"

Her blue gaze lifted, trouble churning within.

"It was my fault that my brother was there. Father had no say over Reginald but he'd forbidden my brother from going off to the prizefight and he kept him close that night. Meanwhile, I borrowed my brother's coats and trousers and followed Reginald." She took in a shaky breath. "When he discovered me missing, Father sent my brother and a servant to retrieve me. Once they'd found me, Amsden thanked me for helping him escape, packed me up with the servant and sent me home." She bit her lip. "It was my fault he was there."

His stomach knotted and twisted. His guilt was so much worse than merely getting her brother killed. He'd set a wolf like Dempsey into an innocent girl's home. "Did Dempsey encourage you to follow him to the inn where he planned to lodge that night?

She looked away and froze. "No."

"Did Amsden?"

She turned toward him and blinked. "He brought me his clothing."

"And saw that your father became aware of your absence." He squeezed her hand. "It wasn't your fault."

She studied her hand knotted with his.

"Your brother was older than you, Jane. He found a way to get himself to that mill, and he made the choice to stay."

She nodded.

"And yet your father lashed out at you."

"Yes." She breathed the word out.

"Then he discovered you were carrying Dempsey's child."

She swallowed hard. "In the midst of haranguing me yet again, he suffered an apoplexy." Trembling, she choked in a breath and pain sketched a deep line between her eyes. "He died in his study, in front of me."

"You can't blame yourself for that," he said.

"How can I not? No matter what my brother did to get away that night, I had already been reckless with Reginald." She squeezed his hand. "So, you see, you must put aside your self-blaming. You may not have always been the invincible Spy Lord, but in this matter, you bear no guilt."

He swiped a thumb across her cheek, the small movement of his muscles snaking up his arm and making his shoulder throb. She no doubt was aching from her wound also. They would both need to rest soon.

She could not travel across town, not in this state.

"I failed Dempsey that day, and your brother, and you." And that failure had driven him, had made him harder, colder. "And I'm sorry, Jane. So very sorry. It's no wonder you wanted revenge against me."

Instead of softening, her mouth firmed. "Revenge? What are you talking about? That's your compulsion, not mine, Shaldon. And don't pity me. I *abhor* pity."

"Pity you?" She was still fighting the inevitable, dear Jane. "There is nothing pitiable about you."

She shook her head and her laugh sounded forced.

"It's true. You're beautiful, and intriguing."

"What rubbish. I am not beautiful, Shaldon, nor intriguing, except for my secrets, which you wanted to winkle out of me as relentlessly as you do with everyone else." She squeezed her eyes shut. "And now you know them. My foolishness brought about my brother's death, my father's death, and left that young man not much better than a foundling."

He leaned in and gathered her close, ignoring his pains. "You caused no one's death, and Penderbrook grew up well cared for, perhaps even a bit spoiled. I am relentless only with enemies, and there I've failed far too often."

"And sought revenge. Oh yes, I know about your efforts against the marquess who plagued Paulette, and Sirena's villainous cousin, and Graciela's despicable guardian. You've been on a quest for revenge."

"Not revenge. Justice." He put a finger under her chin and raised it. Tears glistened but her gaze was clear-eyed.

"Be honest, Jane. Is not revenge part of the reason you stole the painting?"

"No." She bit her lip. "Well perhaps, in the deep recesses of my heart. But Perry told me it was to have been her inheritance, and she didn't want it, and..." She took in a deep breath. "I needed to help my son."

By God, he loved her.

"Is this the end, Shaldon? Will the Duque's loss of a toe at my hands be enough to avenge you?"

He wanted to laugh. The Duque would find being shot by a woman humiliating.

But was it enough?

"The Duque cut you."

"And I shot him."

"We could have the Duquesa spread the tale through her father's people." He stroked her cheek again. That would not be enough for him.

"You're frowning, Shaldon. You must not seek to avenge the Duque's assault on me. You must be satisfied with his toe."

"Must I be?"

She sighed. "You must put the past aside, live in the present, look to the future. You're alive. You've won. And you still have the painting he coveted. Did your men bring along Guignard's copy?"

"The one you brought with you today disappeared from the field of battle. Captain Kingsley saw the Duque's man stuff it inside his coat."

A frown creased her brow. "I meant him to pay me for it. It was a very fair copy. Will he be crowing that he has won back the original, do you think?"

"And sailing off on another chase for sunken treasure? Probably. Perhaps Captain Kingsley would like to raise his privateer flag and follow him. I'd stand him the cost of a ship for that endeavor."

She eased in a breath and her gaze finally softened. More hair had slipped out of her braid, and the thin lawn of her nightgown clung to her breasts.

"Devil take the Duque and the painting," he said. "The original is here in the vault and it is yours. Sell it, give it away, do what you wish with it."

He owed her that, he owed her that for all he'd taken from her. Let it be a revenge against him, whether she wanted vengeance or not.

He pressed his lips to her neck and breathed in her clean smell. "If I put the past behind me, will you come with me into the future? I want that very much. I want *you* very much."

HIS KISS SENT A SHIVER THROUGH HER, HIS LATE-DAY BEARD scratching her jaw and the gape of his banyan revealing dark chest hair laced with gray. She settled a hand there, over his pounding heart.

He was alive, and virile, and no small prize, this man. He knew the worst of her failings, and he claimed he wanted her still.

And God help her, she wanted him also.

Could they both truly leave the past behind them?

She felt her belt loosening, and his hands, large and hot, slipped around her waist, under the robe.

"Shaldon, I...I don't want the Duque or his minions bothering us or any of our children ever again."

"*Our* children." He kissed her cheek. "I like the sound of that."

His grin sent warmth buzzing through her, but she held him off, thinking.

The Duque wanted the painting because he wanted the treasure.

"Did Captain Kingsley discover the painting's treasure?"

"Kingsley and I have both been too busy to talk."

When she turned her head, his stubble rasped against her lips. "Shaldon, your condition…"

He drew her to her feet and pulled her against him, smiling down at her.

He was aroused, in spite of his injuries and a night without sleep, and very proud of it.

She laughed and shook her head. "Good heavens."

A warm hand came around the outside of her robe and began working her plait loose. "Yes, good heavens. Now, what is your answer? I've offered you solid employment and a home."

"*Employment?*"

"Running the Shaldon domestic empire, I believe is how Lady Bakeley sees it. She will gladly surrender the burden." His hand worked the last of her hair free and he lifted a hank and sniffed deeply. "And in payment, my lady, I'll give you my name and my worldly goods, at least those that are not entailed. And the painting of course."

When he brushed her arm, pain shot through her.

He dropped his hand, frowning. "The damn Duque shall—"

"No." She touched his cheek and made him look at her. "No, Shaldon. You are finished with the Duque. Leave the matter of vengeance to me."

Frowning, he leaned in to nuzzle her neck. "What are you planning? Will you shoot off another ducal toe?"

"No weapons will be employed."

He studied her a long moment. "I am enchanted, my lady. Very well. Besides my name and my worldly goods, my heart, my honor, and the rest of my life, vengeance is yours."

"And the painting."

"Of course."

A smile lit his face, and he took her elbow, leading her back to his bedchamber.

And she went.

EPILOGUE

On a rainy morning a few days later, Jane sat next to Shaldon in the front pew of the Bavarian Chapel on Warwick Street, her hand resting in his.

Her arm still ached from her wound, as did Shaldon's shoulder from his injury. But after a day and a half of rest, Shaldon had stopped urging her to stay abed and had proclaimed that he himself was recovered enough to go out.

When he'd disappeared from their bedchamber to set his own plans in motion, she'd summoned Fox, Bakeley, and Lloyd, and finalized her own.

Today, Shaldon watched the proceedings impassively.

Or so everyone would think, everyone who didn't know him as she did. His hooded eyes sparkled at the events transpiring, and one could almost discern excitement in the way he glanced once or twice at his timepiece.

When she squeezed his hand, his lips twitched.

A long prayer in Latin brought his attention back to the altar. Accompanied by close family and friends in this small private ceremony, Charley and Graciela received the blessings of the Roman Church upon their marriage, as well as those of Graciela's father, Captain Kingsley. It had been the Captain's only requirement for final approval of the union, one he insisted was necessary to honor his late wife.

No WEDDING BREAKFAST FOLLOWED, BUT LATER THAT evening, the family and close friends, plus a few carefully selected notable gossips of the *ton* gathered for dinner at Shaldon House. The distant cousin who had performed Charley and Gracie's Anglican wedding was present. Jane's cousin, Lord Cheswick also joined them, appearing by himself, his wife claiming illness. Cheswick allowed the introduction to Quentin, and Jane was happy to see him speak cordially with her son.

In a rare lack of protocol, La Fanelle and Barton also sat down to dinner with them. Shaldon had invited them, in deference to Jane, and probably in part as a poke at his old friend, Kincaid. La Fanelle had wisely been seated down the table from the Scotsman.

When they reached the dessert course, Captain Kingsley toasted the bride and groom, and Charley spoke, and then each of his brothers.

And then Kincaid rose.

Jane gazed down the table where Shaldon sat and caught his eye. He sent her a rare public smile.

"To Charley and Graciela," Kincaid said. "May the best you've ever seen, be the worst you'll ever see." Glasses clinked all around, but instead of sitting, Kincaid beckoned for more drinks to be poured.

"Now." He cleared his throat. "We come to another matter. Lord Shaldon, 'tis said that a righteous heart makes a beautiful character and a harmonious home. And a harmonious home will give order to the nation, and that in turn, my friends, will make for a peaceful world."

"Get on with it," Shaldon said.

Kincaid grinned. "Aye, so I will. My friends, raise a cup to a righteous heart and a beautiful character who will bring peace to the Earl of Shaldon's world. To Lady Jane Montfort, as of this afternoon, the new Countess of Shaldon."

The warm gaze of her husband stretched the length of the table drawing all of her attention—though she was swimming in surprised congratulations and good wishes. A handkerchief was pressed into her hand.

Blast it, she was weeping.

And she must not. She had things to say.

She dabbed at her eyes and nodded to Lloyd.

Two footmen carried in an easel with a draped canvas and placed it near her. She stood and signaled everyone to remain seated.

Shaldon, of course, didn't obey. While the footmen worked, he sauntered down the table to stand beside her, his eyes gleaming.

"I have another announcement," she said. "And your duty, each of you here tonight, is to share this news far and wide."

Lloyd brought a salver with a letter, presenting it to Shaldon.

He picked it up and raised an eyebrow. "It has been opened."

"Of course," she said. "You have a wife now, my lord."

The guests burst into laughter.

"The King's seal—broken" he said, clearing his throat and unfolding the paper with a flourish. He held it at arm's length and studied the short message.

"What does the King say, Father?" Charley called out. "We are waiting with bated breath."

Shaldon raised his eyes and his level gaze held hers.

"Word will be carried to the clubs tonight, and will appear in tomorrow's papers," she whispered. "He will be livid."

"Or the King will be," he murmured.

"No. Fox and Bakeley met with the King and his advisor, Sir Charles Long, to review the provenance. His Majesty found the story of the painting—and the treasure—enthralling." She leaned closer. "The whole story."

"I see."

"It is mine, you said, Shaldon. Both the painting and the revenge."

She held her breath while he studied her, his gaze growing warmer, his lips finally twitching.

He nodded to Lloyd, and the curtain came off.

Guests further down the table leaned sideways or turned in their chairs for a look.

Fox had performed miracles cleaning and refurbishing the painting, a task he said he'd wanted to do ten years earlier for the first Lady Shaldon. The figures crouched in darkness but caught the unearthly glow of the paradise they would soon enter. It was exquisite.

Shaldon lifted the letter again and read. "His Majesty will be pleased to accept the gift to him of the priceless Spanish masterpiece, The Martyrdom of Saints Felicity and Perpetua, by Sebastian Lopez de Arteaga, in honor of his coronation." He passed the parchment to Lloyd and reached for Jane, studying her.

Some of the guests rose and left the table, crowding closer to view the canvas.

Shaldon drew her aside. "*This* is my revenge?" he asked.

"Indeed it is. As I said, the Duque will be livid. He will not try to wrest it from the King of England. And no weapons were needed."

A long moment passed, a smile blooming on his lips. "Remind me never to cross you, my lady."

He wrapped her in his good arm and pressed his lips to hers for a long moment that brought a hush to the room.

Straightening he peered down at her. "Shall we retire?"

Cheeks burning, she nodded.

"Do enjoy the rest of the evening," he said to the rest of the company. "Lady Shaldon and I are beginning our honeymoon."

The End

IF YOU ENJOYED THIS STORY, PLEASE CONSIDER LEAVING A REVIEW at Goodreads, Bookbub, or the bookseller of your choice.

A NOTE FROM THE AUTHOR

Lady Jane Montfort first made an appearance in *The Viscount's Seduction* and I knew immediately that she would be a perfect match for Lord Shaldon, once I got all of his children out of the way. I hope you've enjoyed this "mature" romance—because really, love is ageless!

In 1821 when this story was set, dueling was illegal, but gentlemen still engaged in the practice to settle disputes of honor. My favorite resource on the topic is an 1836 book called *The Art of Dueling*, by "A Traveler". You can download it free from GoogleBooks.

As usual, my characters and story are entirely fictional, and any historical errors are mine alone.

Many thanks go to editor Tessa Shapcott, and as ever, I'm grateful to my husband for his unfailing support and enduring patience.

I love hearing from readers! You can contact and follow me on Facebook, Twitter, Pinterest, and Goodreads, and at my website, https://AlinaKField.com. For special notices about sales and other news, please consider signing up for my newsletter at my website. I promise I won't spam you or sell your email address!

Best regards and happy reading!

Alina K. Field

BOOKS BY ALINA K. FIELD

Sons of the Spy Lord Series

Marrying Mr. Gibson

Previously titled *The Bastard's Iberian Bride*

Paulette Heardwyn rushes to visit her dying guardian, set on learning the truth about her father. But the only man with answers takes his secrets to the grave, leaving her penniless—unless she marries his illegitimate son.

https://alinakfield.com/book/marrying-mr-gibson/

The Viscount's Seduction

Lady Sirena Hollister has lost everything, even her fey abilities. But when the fairies hand her a chance at a London Season, her schemes for revenge stir up an unknown enemy, and spark danger of a different sort, in the person of a handsome Viscount.

https://alinakfield.com/book/the-viscounts-seduction/

The Rogue's Last Scandal

Falling—literally—into the arms of the *ton*'s most outrageous rogue seems a risky path of escape, but Maria Graciela Kingsley y Romero has no other choice. Only England's greatest spy lord can help her, and he is not to be found—so his son will have to do!

https://alinakfield.com/book/rogues-last-scandal/

The Counterfeit Lady

Vowing she'll never submit to an arranged marriage, an earl's daughter bolts for the seaside cottage that will someday be hers. But she finds her quiet refuge occupied by the last man she ever wants to see—an American artist, who's also a thief. And quite possibly one of her father's spies.

https://alinakfield.com/book/the-counterfeit-lady/

Avenging the Earl's Lady

The long war is over, but honor requires vanquishing one last enemy, and the Earl of Shaldon has no time for romance. But when the lady he longs for interferes in his plot, and his enemy strikes at her, nothing else matters but avenging his lady.

https://alinakfield.com/book/avenging-the-earls-lady/

Novellas and Holiday Stories

The Marquess and the Midwife

Finalist, 2016 National Reader's Choice Award

Uncovering a lie drives a new marquess back from a self-imposed exile at Christmas to find the only woman he's ever loved. Finding her turns out to be easy, uncovering her stunning secrets, a bit harder. But winning her back will be the greatest challenge of all.

https://alinakfield.com/book/the-marquess-and-the-midwife/

A Leap Into Love

Can a gentleman be too charming?

The ladies of Upper Upton think so.

When the single ladies of the village conspire to teach their charmer a lesson that might bankrupt him, the town's loveliest young widow—who's sworn off marriage forever—steps up to warn him.

https://alinakfield.com/book/a-leap-into-love/

Liliana's Letter

The Matchmaker Meets the Matchbreaker

Liliana Ashford's future as a professional chaperone depends on her wealthy charge's successful marriage, but her own close encounter with a scoundrel years ago makes her determined to save the girl from the same kind of rogue.

https://alinakfield.com/book/lilianas-letter/

The Ghost of Deplored Hall

A sweet Halloween short story

It's her mother's last All Hallows' Eve.

When family, friends, and tenants gather, goblins, ghouls, and ghosts are banned from this All Hallows' Eve party.

Only, no one told the Ghost of Depford Hall!

https://alinakfield.com/book/ghost-depford-hall/

Courted by the Earl

previously titled *Bella's Band*

A 2015 RONE Award Finalist

Saddled with his brother's title and debts, nothing about this new life makes the Earl of Hackwell want to stay—until he meets a lady with a secret that can change everything.

https://alinakfield.com/book/courted-by-the-earl/

Rosalyn's Ring

2014 Book Buyer's Best Winner, Novella Category

Done with grieving her losses, a late nobleman's daughter has fallen into a tidy spinster's life in London. But when one snowy Christmas Eve, a young woman needs rescue, she seizes the chance to do good—and to recover a family heirloom that ought to be hers.

https://alinakfield.com/book/rosalyns-ring/

Haunting Miss Fenwick

Thrilled to finally have a permanent home, a Squire's daughter won't let a supernatural creature scare her away. While hunting the ghost she doesn't believe in, she stumbles upon a mysterious flesh and blood man who might be the key to all of her problems.

https://alinakfield.com/book/haunting-miss-fenwick/

Lady Twisden's Picture Perfect Match

Promised York's marriage mart and the hospitality of his cousin's doddering stepmother, Major August Kellborn is shocked to find that his fetching hostess is the one woman who stirs his heart.

https://alinakfield.com/book/lady-twisdens-picture-perfect-match/

Flowers for His Lady

Eleanor Gurnwood has only one goal in sight: to make this year's Christmas service beautiful for the parishioners of St. Tancred's—until the Christmas eve when a man from her past rides in on a white horse. https://alinakfield.com/book/flowers-for-his-lady/

Under the Champagne Moon

Homeless and living on the charity of her former guardian, Fleur Hardouin's heart longs for Captain Gareth Ardleigh, whose kindness to her as a child she's never forgotten, but she needs an advantageous marriage.

Gareth has promised to find Fleur—on behalf of another man. Now he must choose between honoring a promise and trying to win the hand of the woman he loves.

https://alinakfield.com/book/under-the-champagne-moon/

The Upstart Christmas Brides Series

The Duke She Despised

Hiding her true identity, a young vicar's widow takes a position as housekeeper in a remote Scottish castle at Christmas for a new duke who years ago sabotaged her chance for happiness. She quickly falls for the duke's charming but not very competent factor, not knowing that he's hiding something also—he's the duke she despised!

https://alinakfield.com/book/the-duke-she-despised/

Convincing the Countess

A penniless widowed countess with trade in her blood descends upon the country manor of her sons' negligent guardian, intent on confronting him about her boys' futures. Instead, she finds his younger brother, a business-minded aristocrat with a penchant for widows and a distaste for emotional entanglements. A man who once witnessed her greatest humiliation. A man offering enticing distractions that threaten to derail all her plans.

https://alinakfield.com/book/convincing-the-countess/

The Impetuous Heiress

Before dashing Lord Loughton can make amends with his neglected fiancée, the lady's meddling cousin delivers her to his doorstep. He soon realizes more is amiss than his carelessness. Can he uncover her secrets and win her back before he loses her altogether?

https://alinakfield.com/book/the-impetuous-heiress/

The Nabob's Designing Daughter

Ripped from his prestigious London practice to deliver a Highland duke's heir, a young doctor finds there are more snares awaiting than a risky birth, including a surprise—and worthless—bequest. There's also his best friend's cousin, who's blossomed from mousey to heart-stirringly beautiful, with enough wiles to convince an ambitious man that his heart belongs in the Highlands.

https://alinakfield.com/book/the-nabobs-designing-daughter/

The Earl's Scottish Hoyden

Coerced by her brother to spend an English Christmas at the country estate of the handsome but cold earl who all but jilted her a year earlier, Edme Beecham is determined to do no more than assist her brother in his business negotiations with the earl, and by all means, to protect her heart.

https://alinakfield.com/book/the-earls-scottish-hoyden/

The Macbeth Series

Fated Hearts

A Love After All Retelling of the Scottish Play

A Scottish Baron returning from two decades at war meets the wife he divorced and the daughter he disavowed before she was born, only to learn that everything he'd believed was a lie. Determined to win back the only woman he's ever loved he must first face the viper who drove them apart.

https://alinakfield.com/book/fated-hearts/

The Comtesse of Midnight

A Scottish Earl on a quest for the elusive Comtesse de Fontenay, rescues a French lady smuggler during a devastating storm, taking shelter with her. As the stormy night drags on, he suspects she knows the lady he's seeking, the lady who holds the secret to his identity.

https://alinakfield.com/book/the-comtesse-of-midnight/

Claims of the Heart

Since a perilous fall, Lucie Macbeth has been seeing more than a settled future as the heiress to a Scottish barony. The visions plaguing her include a man—one far above her class and breeding, and English to boot. He's engaged to a duke's granddaughter as well, and thus wholly inappropriate. Though she can't marry him, and she won't become any man's leman, when the Sight warns her of danger to him, her conscience, and her heart tell her she can't walk away.

https://alinakfield.com/book/claims-of-the-heart/